INTRODUCING ISSUES WITH OPPOSING VIEWPOINTS®

Obesity

Other books in the Introducing Issues with Opposing Viewpoints series:

Advertising
AIDS
Alcohol
Animal Rights
Civil Liberties
Cloning
The Death Penalty
Drug Abuse
Drunk Driving
Energy Alternatives
The Environment
Euthanasia
Gangs
Gay Marriage
Genetic Engineering
Global Warming
Gun Control
Islam
Military Draft
Racism
Smoking
Teen Pregnancy
Terrorism
UFOs

INTRODUCING ISSUES WITH OPPOSING VIEWPOINTS®

Obesity

Sandra Alters, *Book Editor*

Christine Nasso, *Publisher*
Elizabeth Des Chenes, *Managing Editor*

GREENHAVEN PRESS
An imprint of Thomson Gale, a part of The Thomson Corporation

THOMSON
GALE

Detroit • New York • San Francisco • New Haven, Conn. • Waterville, Maine • London

THOMSON
GALE

For more information, contact
Greenhaven Press
27500 Drake Rd.
Farmington Hills, MI 48331-3535
Or you can visit our Internet site at http://www.gale.com

Articles in Greenhaven Press anthologies are often edited for length to meet page requirements. In addition, original titles of these works are changed to clearly present the main thesis and to explicitly indicate the author's opinion. Every effort is made to ensure that Greenhaven Press accurately reflects the original intent of the authors.

Every effort has been made to trace the owners of copyrighted material.

LIBRARY OF CONGRESS CATALOGING-IN-PUBLICATION DATA

Obesity / Sandra Alters, book editor.
p. cm. — (Introducing issues with opposing viewpoints)
Includes bibliographical references and index.
ISBN-13: 978-0-7377-3545-1 (hardcover : alk. paper)
ISBN-10: 0-7377-3545-7 (hardcover : alk. paper)
1. Obesity. I. Alters, Sandra.
RC628.O2155 2006
616.3'98—dc22

2006030386

Printed in the United States of America

Contents

Foreword

Indulging in a wide spectrum of ideas, beliefs, and perspectives is a critical cornerstone of democracy. After all, it is often debates over differences of opinion, such as whether to legalize abortion, how to treat prisoners, or when to enact the death penalty, that shape our society and drive it forward. Such diversity of thought is frequently regarded as the hallmark of a healthy and civilized culture. As the Reverend Clifford Schutjer of the First Congregational Church in Mansfield, Ohio, declared in a 2001 sermon, "Surrounding oneself with only like-minded people, restricting what we listen to or read only to what we find agreeable is irresponsible. Refusing to entertain doubts once we make up our minds is a subtle but deadly form of arrogance." With this advice in mind, Introducing Issues with Opposing Viewpoints books aim to open readers' minds to the critically divergent views that comprise our world's most important debates.

Introducing Issues with Opposing Viewpoints simplifies for students the enormous and often overwhelming mass of material now available via print and electronic media. Collected in every volume is an array of opinions that captures the essence of a particular controversy or topic. Introducing Issues with Opposing Viewpoints books embody the spirit of nineteenth-century journalist Charles A. Dana's axiom: "Fight for your opinions, but do not believe that they contain the whole truth, or the only truth." Absorbing such contrasting opinions teaches students to analyze the strength of an argument and compare it to its opposition. From this process readers can inform and strengthen their own opinions, or be exposed to new information that will change their minds. Introducing Issues with Opposing Viewpoints is a mosaic of different voices. The authors are statesmen, pundits, academics, journalists, corporations, and ordinary people who have felt compelled to share their experiences and ideas in a public forum. Their words have been collected from newspapers, journals, books, speeches, interviews, and the Internet, the fastest growing body of opinionated material in the world.

Introducing Issues with Opposing Viewpoints shares many of the well-known features of its critically acclaimed parent series, Opposing Viewpoints. The articles are presented in a pro/con format, allowing readers to absorb divergent perspectives side by side. Active reading questions preface each viewpoint, requiring the student to approach the material thoughtfully and carefully. Useful charts, graphs, and cartoons supplement each article. A thorough introduction provides readers with crucial background on an issue. An annotated bibliography points the reader toward articles, books, and Web sites that contain additional information on the topic. An appendix of organizations to contact contains a wide variety of charities, nonprofit organizations, political groups, and private enterprises that each hold a position on the issue at hand. Finally, a comprehensive index allows readers to locate content quickly and efficiently.

Introducing Issues with Opposing Viewpoints is also significantly different from Opposing Viewpoints. As the series title implies, its presentation will help introduce students to the concept of opposing viewpoints, and learn to use this material to aid in critical writing and debate. The series' four-color, accessible format makes the books attractive and inviting to readers of all levels. In addition, each viewpoint has been carefully edited to maximize a reader's understanding of the content. Short but thorough viewpoints capture the essence of an argument. A substantial, thought-provoking essay question placed at the end of each viewpoint asks the student to further investigate the issues raised in the viewpoint, compare and contrast two authors' arguments, or consider how one might go about forming an opinion on the topic at hand. Each viewpoint contains sidebars that include at-a-glance information and handy statistics. A Facts About section located in the back of the book further supplies students with relevant facts and figures.

Following in the tradition of the Opposing Viewpoints series, Greenhaven Press continues to provide readers with invaluable exposure to the controversial issues that shape our world. As John Stuart Mill once wrote: "The only way in which a human being can make some approach to knowing the whole of a subject is by hearing what can be said about it by persons of every variety of opinion and studying all modes in which it can be looked at by every character of mind. No wise man ever acquired his wisdom in any mode but this." It is to this principle that Introducing Issues with Opposing Viewpoints books are dedicated.

Introduction

"As the world's wealthiest nation, the United States is also building the biggest bodies. It's hardly cause for patriotic pride."

—Craig Lambert, author

The World Health Organization reports that obesity is a global epidemic. More than 1 billion adults worldwide are overweight or obese. Percentages of overweight and obese individuals vary among countries, but the United States leads the world. In 2004, according to the Organization for Economic Cooperation and Development (OECD), 65 percent of the U.S. population was overweight or obese. In contrast, countries with the lowest proportion of their populations overweight or obese were France and Switzerland (37 percent), Korea (35 percent) and Japan (26 percent). That the United States has become the fattest nation in the world is a troubling fact that raises a critical question about American society: Does it promote obesity?

It has been well documented that both the condition of being overweight and being obese have multiple, complex causes. Genetics can play a factor, as can a person's natural metabolism and even economic status. A simple cause, however, is one that many people already know: Being overweight and obese results in part from eating too much and exercising too little. A close look at many aspects of U.S. culture reveals that the American lifestyle can often steer Americans toward a sedentary and high-calorie routine.

Eating quickly or on the go is a negative American eating habit that has become increasingly common. Crunched for time, many people grab food to eat as they are walking, driving, or doing another activity in transit. In fact, the habit of eating quickly or eating while doing something else frequently causes people to unwittingly overeat. The Weight Control Information Network explains, "Eating while doing other things makes it easy to lose track of how much you've already eaten." In countries with relatively low percentages of overweight and obese populations, such as France and Japan, people tend to avoid

The United States is the fattest nation in the world. Sixty-five percent of its population is overweight or obese.

eating on the go; instead, they eat slowly and savor not only their food but also the experience of eating. In fact, cup holders, a standard feature in American cars, cannot even be found in Japanese cars. The American habit of "dashboard dining" is certainly one way in which people tend to eat quickly or to overeat.

The automobile not only doubles as an American dining room, but it is also a place where Americans expend few calories while they sit—for up to hours each day—behind the wheel. In a 2004 study by the University of California at Berkeley that examined how Americans spend their time, researchers found that the number-one activity in American culture is driving a car. One explanation for the automobile-centered society is the shift that occurred during the twentieth century from an urban to a suburban culture. Land in the suburbs tends to be less expensive than in the city, and the extra space attracts families that want their kids to be able to play in a private yard. But living in the suburbs means driving almost everywhere: to work, to school, to shopping, and to entertainment. In addition, some urban areas have become sprawling and huge, making walking to work, school, shopping, and entertainment difficult or impossible.

The second most common activity found by the 2004 study is job-related office work. Indeed, the long American workweek results in Americans spending a great number of hours sitting behind desks. Americans spend more hours working than people in many other countries. The OECD determined that in 2004, for example, Americans spent 1,777 hours working each year, but in France and Germany people spent only 1,350 hours working per year. Working long hours in sedentary jobs not only contributes to the inadequate physical activity of Americans but also to excess consumption of fat and calories. Employees may snack at their desks to pass the time or may be pushed toward grabbing prepackaged or fast foods. When

"Dashboard dining" has become an increasingly common habit among Americans. People who eat in their car tend to overeat and eat quickly.

both parents in a family work and no one is at home to prepare meals, the push toward eating out is even stronger. Today more than 60 percent of married women with young children work outside the home, and 39 percent work in full-time jobs, according to the opinion research organization Public Agenda. The researchers of the University of California at Berkeley study said the high rates of car and office time in America "presented a graphic portrait of a society in which sedentary and low-intensity activities predominate."

Komarnitski. Reproduced by permission of Cagle Cartoons, Inc.

The high level of modernization the country enjoys further contributes to Americans' low level of activity. Elevators and escalators found in most buildings passively transport people, and automatic doors don't even require a push to open. Modern appliances wash dishes, clothes, and vacuum the floors instead of requiring a person to work. Indeed, previous generations expended hundreds of calories doing chores that now need only the push of a button. "We've engineered activity out of daily life," says Steven Blair of the Cooper Institute for Aerobics Research in Dallas. Though modern technology has made life infinitely more convenient, it has also cut down on the opportunity to be active during the day.

Thus, modern Americans must make time to exercise—and in an increasingly busy world, this can be harder and harder to do. The Centers for Disease Control and Prevention suggest that people find a balance between sedentary and physical activity and exercise for at least thirty minutes most days of the week. The increasing popularity of gyms—even those that are open for twenty-four hours—might further help Americans fit exercise into their busy but sedentary lifestyles. What factors might contribute to and help reduce obesity are just two of the fascinating and important topics explored in *Introducing Issues with Opposing Viewpoints: Obesity.*

Chapter 1

Is Obesity a Serious Health Problem?

An obese woman eats chicken from a fast food restaurant while sitting outside a London hospital.

Viewpoint 1

Obesity Is a Major Health Problem

Centers for Disease Control and Prevention

"Fighting obesity is one way our nation could substantially cut . . . costs of the nation's three leading killers."

The following viewpoint, published by the Centers for Disease Control and Prevention (CDC), describes the health risks associated with obesity. The CDC contends that obesity is dangerous because it can lead to diabetes, cardiovascular disease, and cancer, the three leading killers in the United States. According to the CDC, decreasing weight and increasing activity levels could fight all three diseases.

The Centers for Disease Control and Prevention is a governmental agency charged with protecting the health and safety of Americans.

AS YOU READ, CONSIDER THE FOLLOWING QUESTIONS:

1. What was the rate of obesity in the United States in 2003?
2. What are three of the cancers associated with obesity?
3. Regarding obesity, what were the findings of an August 2004 Zogby International Poll?

"Target Obesity and Bring Down the Big Three: Cancer, Cardiovascular Disease, and Diabetes," *Chronic Disease Notes & Reports*, Centers for Disease Control and Prevention, www.cdc.gov, 14 Winter 2005.

Obesity has been linked to many life-threatening diseases, including cancer, heart disease, and diabetes.

Cancer, cardiovascular disease, and diabetes caused about 65% of deaths in the United States during 2000. Their common risk factor? Obesity.

The prevalence of obesity in the United States increased from 20.9% in 2001 to 22.2% in 2003, according to data from the Behavioral Risk Factor Surveillance System. Fighting obesity is one way our nation could substantially cut the human and economic costs of the nation's three leading killers, said a recent statement issued jointly by the American Cancer Society, the American Diabetes Association, and the American Heart Association. . . .

Obesity Leads to Diabetes

Currently, an estimated 18.2 million Americans have diabetes, and there are about 1.3 million new cases per year. Most people with type 2 diabetes are obese, and most of them die of some form of heart or blood vessel disease. "Diabetes increases the risk for heart disease and stroke so much that a diagnosis is considered a step up in the risk of having a first heart attack," said CDC epidemiologist Rodolfo Valdez.

Happily, losing a little weight, even 5%–10% of one's starting weight, can help people prevent or delay the onset of diabetes. CDC scientists and colleagues at the National Institutes of Health recently studied more than 3,200 adults over age 25 who were at increased risk of developing type 2 diabetes. Their blood glucose or sugar was higher than normal, but not yet high enough to be diabetes. All study participants were overweight, most were obese, and most had a family history of type 2 diabetes.

The study results showed that a healthy diet, exercise, and losing a little weight can prevent or delay the disease. More than 10 million

A diabetic girl injects herself with insulin to control her blood sugar levels. Being overweight increases a person's chance of developing diabetes.

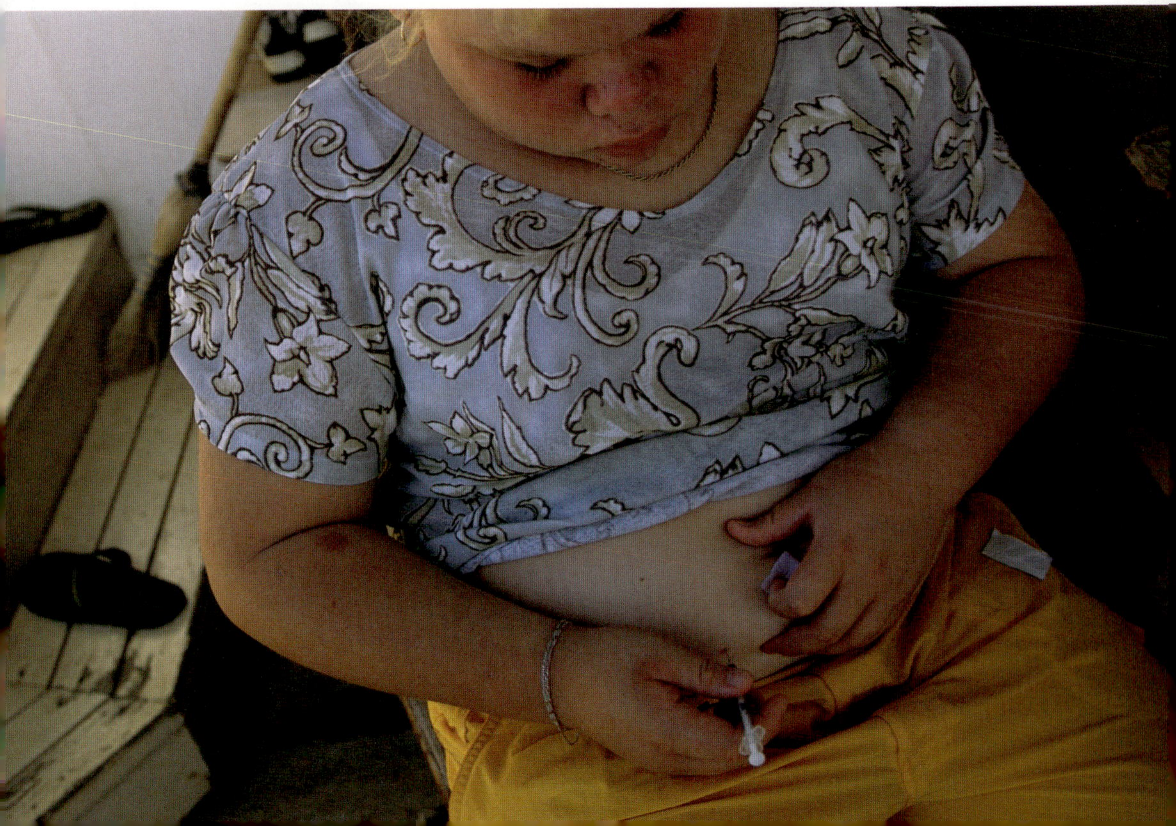

people in the United States have characteristics similar to those of the study participants and thus have an increased risk of developing diabetes.

Obesity's Link with Heart Disease and Stroke

Obesity raises people's risk for cardiovascular disease (CVD), and this "is a major reason for concern about the rising prevalence of obesity," said Darwin Labarthe, CDC's Associate Director for Cardiovascular Health Policy and Research.

Health Risks Associated with Obesity

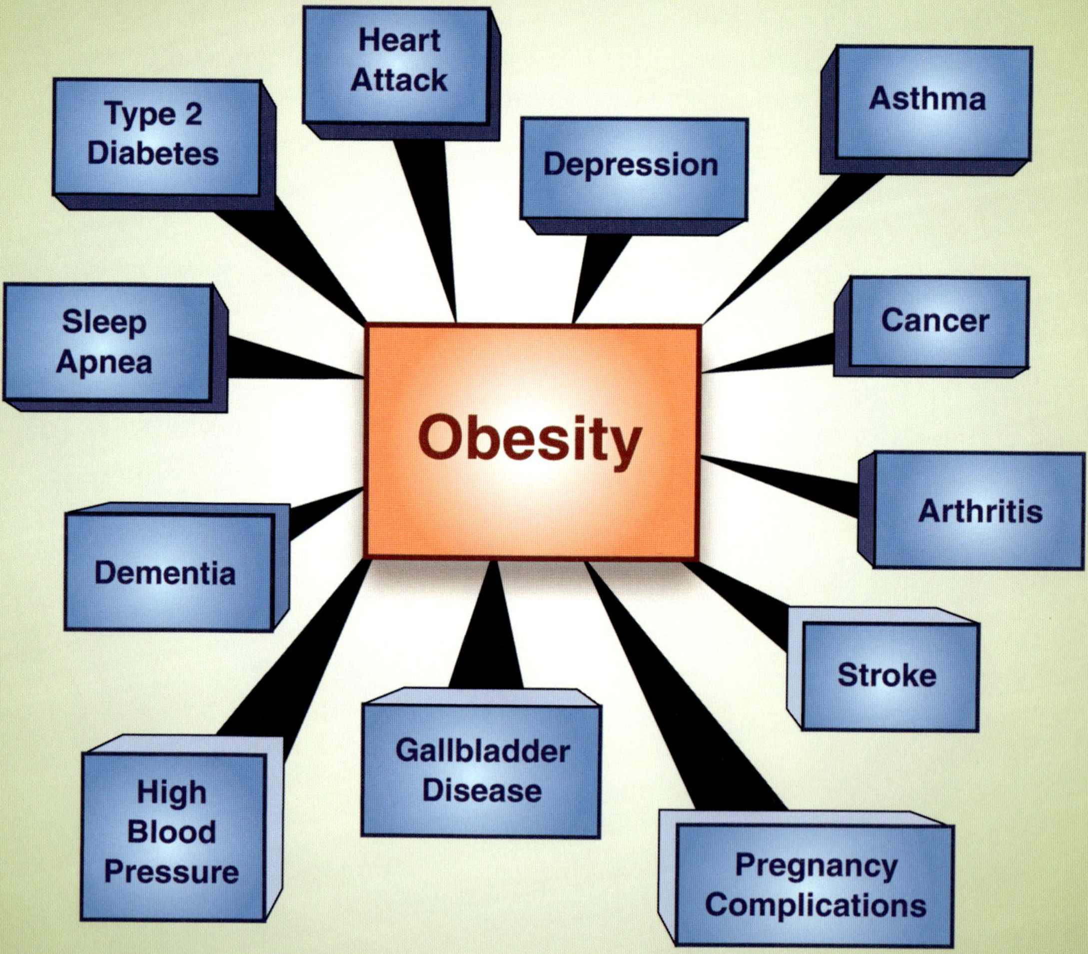

Source: "Overweight and Obesity: Health Consequences," United States Department of Health and Human Services, 2001. www.surgeongeneral.gov/topics/obesity/calltoaction/fact_consequences.html.

Obesity influences all of the major risk factors for CVD, including high blood pressure, high cholesterol and other lipid disorders, and diabetes. Obesity is a good predictor of heart blockage. It also contributes to heart disease by increasing the risk for diabetes. For some people, diabetes makes these other risk factors much worse and thus increases the danger of heart attack.

FAST FACT

According to the World Health Organization, the number of overweight children has doubled and the number of overweight adolescents has tripled since 1980.

Weight loss often eliminates all of these CVD risk factors. The evidence is strong that weight loss reduces one's risk for heart disease and stroke. "From a CVD perspective, we're interested in the impact of weight control," said Dr. Labarthe. "Preventing obesity is a necessary component of strategies to prevent not only heart disease and stroke but their major risk factors as well."

Obesity Linked to Cancer

Being both overweight and physically inactive could account for 25%–30% of several major cancers, according to the International Agency for Research on Cancer. Cancers linked to physical inactivity and overweight are those of the breast (among postmenopausal women), colon, endometrium, kidney, and esophagus. In fact, weight gain during adulthood has been found to be the most consistent and strongest predictor of breast cancer risk.

Researchers believe that physical inactivity and overweight/obesity increase a person's risk for cancer through several different biological pathways. For example, obesity might increase people's risk for breast, endometrium, and prostate cancers by influencing the activity of various hormones in the body. In addition, fat cells release cytokines, proteins that may trigger inflammation, which has been linked to the development of cancer.

Fortunately, getting regular physical activity lowers the risk for colon and breast cancers, and avoiding weight gain can help lower the risk for many cancers. Although researchers are certain about the benefits

Physicians can play an important role in helping patients control their weight so they avoid developing obesity-related diseases.

of avoiding weight gain, they are uncertain whether losing weight reduces a person's risk for these cancers. "It is nonetheless clear that individuals who are overweight or obese should be strongly encouraged and supported in their efforts to reduce their weight," advised the joint statement from the American Cancer Society, the American Diabetes Association, and the American Heart Association.

Doctors Must Help

Despite the clear benefits of lifestyle changes, physicians are sometimes reluctant to advise patients to change their behaviors. "The medical community needs to lead in communicating the importance of physical activity for health and weight maintenance," stated a recent commentary in *JAMA* [Journal of the American Medical Association]. "Just as weight is addressed in some manner at nearly every physician visit, so should attention be given to recommending the accumulation of 30 minutes a day of moderate-intensity physical activity at least 5 days a week." Likewise, the National Institutes of Health recommend that "the health care practitioner needs to heighten a patient's motivation for weight loss and prepare the patient for treatment."

There is some evidence that patients expect their physicians to discuss lifestyle changes. According to CNN [Cable News Network], obesity ranked second among health concerns nationally in an August 2004 poll by Zogby International. Health care costs were the number one concern. The respondents said that physicians should take more pains to promote healthy lifestyles.

EVALUATING THE AUTHOR'S ARGUMENTS:

In the viewpoint you just read, the CDC claims that obesity leads to death from heart disease, cancer, and diabetes. In the next viewpoint, author David Martosko argues that the seriousness of the obesity epidemic is greatly exaggerated. After reading both viewpoints, which one do you find more convincing? Why?

Viewpoint 2

The Problem of Obesity Is Exaggerated

David Martosko

"Our national debate on [obesity] has become nothing short of hysterical."

In the following viewpoint, David Martosko argues that America's obesity problem has been exaggerated. Drug companies, animal rights groups, and lawyers, according to Martosko, inflate the number of deaths related to obesity in order to increase their profits or advocate their cause. Martosko says that they also exaggerate the costs associated with obesity. The author concludes that America has been tricked into thinking it has an obesity problem and urges Americans to think realistically about weight issues.

David Martosko is the director of research for the Center for Consumer Freedom, a nonprofit group of restaurants, food companies, and consumers working together to promote personal responsibility and protect consumer choices, according to its Web site.

AS YOU READ, CONSIDER THE FOLLOWING QUESTIONS:

1. According to Martosko, why do animal rights groups want to frighten the public about obesity?

David Martosko, "Obesity Claims Overstated, Consumer Advocate Tells FDA," *The Heartland Institute*, www.heartland.org, August 1, 2004. Reproduced by permission.

2. Why is it inaccurate to state that three hundred thousand Americans die each year from obesity, according to the author?
3. Name two celebrities who Martosko says would be classified as overweight under new obesity definitions.

Obesity is a genuine problem in America, but our national debate on the subject has become nothing short of hysterical. And around every corner is a hidden agenda.

Trying to Make Money off an Obesity "Problem"

Some pharmaceutical interests, such as the American Obesity Association, are promoting an alarmist view of the problem in order

A spokeswoman for the Center for Science in the Public Interest delivers a lecture on why certain foods should be taxed or banned. Critics complain the organization unfairly demonizes food.

to justify increased government support and promotion of new obesity drugs.

Animal rights groups, like the deceptively named "Physicians Committee for Responsible Medicine," like to inflame the public's fears about the dangers of obesity in order to disparage consumption of beef, chicken, pork, milk, cheese, and other nutritious foods that come from animals.

And then there are radical nutrition activist groups like the Center for Science in the Public Interest (CSPI), which never met a tasty food it couldn't carp about. The leaders of these groups seldom pass up a chance to announce a desire to tax foods they don't like out of ordinary Americans' reach. CSPI has recklessly tried to characterize certain foods as being as risky as tobacco, in deliberate scare campaigns.

Trial lawyers, in turn, are attempting to turn America's love of good food into their next cash cow. And some activists and academics have proposed zoning restrictions and other draconian regulations on restaurants.

Wolverton. Reproduced by permission of Cagle Cartoons, Inc.

Better Science Is Needed

The nation would surely be better served by a serious and scientific approach to addressing obesity. As the Food and Drug Administration builds a framework for messages to the public about weight reduction, it is important to avoid inadvertently exaggerating or misrepresenting the problem. And steering clear of needless hyperbole can be as simple as checking your facts and figures.

The three most commonly cited statistics associated with the obesity epidemic are (1) that obesity causes 300,000 American deaths per year; (2) that 61 percent of Americans are overweight or obese; and (3) that the economic cost of American obesity is $117 billion a year. All three are seriously flawed.

Fast Fact

According to *The Harvard Medical School Family Health Guide*, research shows that persons can be overweight, yet fit, if they exercise.

Death Rates Are Overstated

Let's start with the common belief that 300,000 U.S. deaths each year are attributable to excess weight. The truth is, "the data linking overweight and death . . . are limited, fragmented, and often ambiguous." That's from an editorial by the respected *New England Journal of Medicine* in January 1998 questioning the increasingly frantic rhetoric about obesity as a public health problem.

Speaking specifically about the 300,000 number, the *New England Journal* editorial continued: "[T]hat figure is by no means well established. Not only is it derived from weak or incomplete data, but it is also called into question by the methodological difficulties of determining which of the many factors contribute to premature death."

It turns out that in order to allege that 300,000 Americans die each year from obesity, you would have to claim that everyone who dies while overweight dies because of that excess weight.

Exaggerated Health Costs

Many in government and the mass media have blindly accepted the claim that obesity costs Americans $117 billion per year, believing the figure came from the Surgeon General. But the original source is a single study published in the March 1998 issue of the journal *Obesity Research.*

The *Obesity Research* study has serious limitations, as the authors themselves admit. "We are still uncertain about the actual amount of health utilization associated with overweight and obesity," they wrote, explaining that "height and weight are not included in many of the primary data sources."

Furthermore, the authors of the study defined obesity incorrectly, writing, "The current estimate of the cost of obesity defines obesity

How to Calculate Adult BMI

Body Mass Index is a ratio of weight to height and provides an estimate of body fat. It establishes a point of normal weight, overweight, and obesity.

1. Enter height in inches: ________________
2. Multiply height in inches by itself: ________________
   (For example, if you are 60 inches tall, 60 x 60 = 360)
3. Enter your weight in pounds: ________________
4. Divide your weight by your answer for line 2: ________________
5. Multiply the result by 703: ________________
   This is your BMI.

Example: Mary is 5'4", or 64 inches. Her answer for line two would be 4096. She weighs 185 pounds. Dividing 185 by 4096 results in .0451. Multiplying by 703 results in a BMI of 31.7. Under current standards, Mary would be considered obese.

BMI	Weight Status
Below 18.5	Underweight
18.5–24.9	Normal
25.0–29.9	Overweight
30.0 and Above	Obese

Source: Editor generated chart. Data from Centers for Disease Control.

Although actor Will Smith appears thin and healthy, he is technically obese as defined by some government studies. Critics argue this is proof the studies are flawed.

as a BMI [body mass index] greater than or equal to 29." Obesity is actually defined as a BMI greater than or equal to 30. Thus the *Obesity Research* study erroneously included the economic cost of individuals with a BMI between 29 and 30. That's more than 10 million Americans.

Finally, the authors acknowledged that even if some data flaws were corrected, their methodology would still result in double- or even triple-counting of obesity-related costs. They write, "Our model assumes that coronary heart disease, hypertension, and diabetes occur independently. However, we know that there is some interdependence among these disease states, especially in obese patients." They go on to admit, "calculating the cost of obesity as it related to these diseases independently would inflate the cost estimate."

Flawed Obesity Definition

Are 61 percent of Americans really overweight or obese? Overweight and obesity are diagnosed by using the body mass index (BMI), a deeply flawed standard. According to the Centers for Disease Control and Prevention, "Overweight may or may not be due to increases in body fat. It may also be due to an increase in lean muscle. For example, professional athletes may be very lean and muscular, with very little body fat, yet they may weigh more than others of the same height. While they may qualify as 'overweight' due to their large muscle mass, they are not necessarily 'over fat,' regardless of BMI." This language is taken from the CDC's Web site. It's that agency's official position.

Using the BMI standard, our very fit President, George W. Bush, is officially overweight. And the incredibly fit [Arnold Schwarzenegger] is considered obese.

The group of Americans presently "overweight" includes svelte movie stars such as Will Smith and Brad Pitt. Also "overweight" were Michael Jordan and Cal Ripken Jr. at the height of their athletic powers. And slugger Barry Bonds is "obese."

EVALUATING THE AUTHOR'S ARGUMENTS:

In the previous viewpoint by the CDC, the organization uses statistics to link obesity to serious health problems. The author of this viewpoint, David Martosko, gives a different interpretation of the statistics. Can statistics mean different things? How do you decide who is interpreting statistics most accurately?

Viewpoint 3

Obesity Is a Disease

Steven Findlay

"About 50% to 70% of the tendency toward obesity is inherited."

In the following viewpoint, author Steven Findlay argues that obesity deserves to be designated as a disease. Classifying obesity as a disease would allow obesity treatment to be covered by insurance policies, allowing more obese Americans to get medical help. Findlay reasons that obesity is similar to other diseases, such as heart disease, cancer, and stroke, which are partly caused by lifestyle and environment and partly by genetics. The author concludes that designating obesity as a disease can hasten responses to fighting it.

Steven Findlay is a health policy analyst in Washington, D.C. He wrote this editorial for *USA Today*.

AS YOU READ, CONSIDER THE FOLLOWING QUESTIONS:

1. According to the author, what proportion of Americans are obese today?
2. What is the chance that the children of obese parents will also be obese, as reported by Findlay?
3. In 2003 how many measures were introduced in state legislatures to address the problem of obesity according to the author?

Steven Findlay, "Designate Obesity as Disease," *USA Today*, December 15, 2003, copyright 2003, USA Today. Reproduced by permission of the author.

You have no doubt heard: Obesity is fast becoming public health enemy No. 1. We are big and getting bigger. We have super-sized, fat-snacked and couch-slouched our way to a serious health crisis. This threatens to reverse the hard-won gains we've made during the past 30 years: lower rates of heart-disease deaths, longer life expectancy and healthier aging.

In 1980, about 45% of U.S. adults were overweight or obese. That rose to 55% in 1990. Today, the proportion is 65% (half of whom are obese, meaning about 30 pounds or more above a healthy weight for their height). Yes, an incredible two-thirds of U.S. adults weigh too much. So do many of our children. Fifteen percent of 6- to 19-year-olds—about 9 million—are overweight, up from 10% a decade

Each year, more Americans become overweight or obese, putting a drain on the country's medical resources and increasing rates of heart disease and cancer.

ago. The price tag is about $120 billion a year in medical expenses and lost productivity.

Opinion varies widely about what to do. The newest recommendation came [in December 2003], when a government-convened panel of experts recommended that doctors weigh and measure all their adult patients and refer obese ones to intensive counseling and behavioral treatment.

We Must Declare Obesity a Disease

That's welcome advice, but it falls short of the decisive action needed to kick-start a more serious response to this epidemic: designating obesity as a distinct disease. The IRS did so in 2002, so taxpayers could deduct the cost of weight-loss programs prescribed by a doctor. And federal health officials and private-sector health groups have been reviewing the issue for months. As with alcoholism and drug addiction, this step would permit millions of Americans to get the help they now lack because of limits in public and private insurance coverage. It would put obesity prevention and treatment research and drug development on new footings. And it gradually would alter public perceptions of the condition.

> **FAST FACT**
>
> **In 2004, Medicare, a government-administered health insurance, officially declared obesity to be a disease.**

Although not without controversy, mounting scientific evidence and medical consensus supports the move. Genetics is the foundation. Studies of twins indicate that about 50% to 70% of the tendency toward obesity is inherited. Likewise, studies show that when both parents are obese, the chance their offspring also will be obese is 60% to 80%. In contrast, when both parents are thin, the likelihood of a child becoming obese is 9%.

The emerging theory is that the genetic tendency to obesity is both metabolic and behavioral. In other words, obesity occurs mostly because of disturbances in the body's regulation of fat and calories, but also because of biologically based abnormalities in food cravings, satiety and eating patterns.

Lifestyle Is Part of Other Diseases

Skeptical opponents assert four things: (a) that plain old overeating and inactivity are the chief causes of obesity (even in people with a genetic "propensity"); (b) that the gene pool hasn't changed in the past 20 years, but eating habits have; (c) that not all obese people are unhealthy; and (d) that "medicalizing" obesity will detract from public health efforts focused on individual responsibility for one's weight.

But most diseases today, including heart disease, cancer, stroke and AIDS, are partly if not significantly due to lifestyle and behavioral choices. Obesity is the end result of poor lifestyle and genetics in the same way that lung cancer or heart attacks can be the end result of smoking and genetics. And there's growing evidence that all obese people are at higher risk of premature death, similar to all people who have elevated cholesterol levels, which is declared a medical condition worthy of professional care.

Drawing Lines

All of that said, if and when obesity is deemed a disease, the biggest challenge will be drawing the line between obesity and plain everyday overweight. There's no evidence that the latter is primarily driven by genetics, especially for people who are carrying around an extra 5–7 pounds or so. Today's cutoffs based on the body mass index (BMI) scale are simple and useful, but doctors and insurers will have to make judgments. Clearer guidelines must be set.

Separating the obese from the purely overweight and medically targeting the former does not get us off the hook from more aggressively attacking all of America's excess poundage. There's a raging debate now about who is to blame, and the lawsuit mill has begun. This is mostly a waste of energy and time. We are all to blame: It's a broad social failure, a cultural milieu that backfired, big time.

Everyone Must Take More Responsibility

The larger solution lies in every institution and individual doing his or her part. Some are moving in the right direction. Food companies such as Kraft are pledging to make healthier snacks. Fast-food chains are promising new low-fat choices and say they will alter their

Scientists who study overweight twins have concluded that 50–70 percent of the tendency toward obesity is inherited.

ingredients. Large employers are taking a new look at work-site counseling. Health plans and doctors are initiating new prevention, treatment and weight-management programs. Communities are talking about more walking and bike trails and kids' after-school-activity programs. The Food and Drug Administration is poised to make food labels clearer. State legislators introduced some 150 measures in 2003 addressing the problem, twice 2002's number. Individuals are taking responsibility.

But even larger-scale social action is needed. As with the public-health response to infectious diseases, smoking, auto safety and traffic deaths due to drunken driving, once the evidence becomes clear, we must kick into high gear. That means firm government regulation and changes in behavior, both voluntary and altered by law (think smoking in public places).

The problem is that this process can take years. Declaring obesity a disease would be a strong first step toward accelerating our response

Some fast food restaurants, including this McDonald's in New York City, are beginning to offer healthier menu items such as salads and low-fat sandwiches.

to the epidemic of excess fat in our diets, on our bodies and in our body politic.

We are earth's richest nation and in many ways its most creative. Let's not be its fattest.

EVALUATING THE AUTHOR'S ARGUMENTS:

In this viewpoint, the author argues that designating obesity a disease will help fight the problem. In the next viewpoint, author Stephen D. Ball argues that such a designation might be bad for obese people. After reading both viewpoints, list the pros and cons for obese people if obesity were considered a disease. Do you think obesity should be considered a disease? Why or why not?

Viewpoint 4

Obesity Is Not a Disease

Stephen D. Ball

"I believe it is too premature to declare obesity a disease, and that by doing so, it will only make the situation worse."

In the following viewpoint, nutritionist Stephen D. Ball warns against classifying obesity as a disease. He argues that it is not clear whether obesity is a true disease because it may not be the cause of poor health. In addition, the author suggests that calling obesity a disease may promote unhealthy weight-loss strategies because physicians and patients may focus on weight loss rather than on healthy lifestyles.

Stephen D. Ball holds a doctorate in nutritional sciences and teaches in the College of Human Environmental Sciences at the University of Missouri at Columbia.

AS YOU READ, CONSIDER THE FOLLOWING QUESTIONS:

1. According to this viewpoint, how much money is spent on weight-loss products and promotions each year?
2. According to studies conducted at the Cooper Institute, what is the best indicator of mortality? What bearing does this have on whether obesity causes poor health?
3. According to Ball, why are practices that promote fast weight loss, such as diet pills and radical diets, considered unhealthy?

Stephen D. Ball, "Is Obesity a Disease?" Missouri Families, http://missourifamilies.org. Reproduced by permission of the author.

There is little question that Americans are getting fatter despite one third of all adults trying to lose weight at any given time. A staggering 30 billion dollars are being spent annually on weight loss products and promotions, yet as a nation we are gaining weight at an unprecedented rate. Some statistics report that approximately half of all adults in this country can be considered overweight and nearly one third can be classified as obese. Childhood obesity has also doubled in the last 20 years. These epidemic proportions have forced the medical community, fitness and health professionals, dieticians, and government agencies to "wage a war on obesity." Former President [Bill] Clinton was even encouraged to declare obesity a national health crisis and in 1998 the World Health Organization officially declared obesity a disease.

The Danger of Classifying Obesity as a Disease

Currently there is a heated debate within the fitness and health care professions over the classification of obesity as a disease. There is little question that obesity is associated with a variety of negative health

Because it is unclear the extent to which being overweight causes health problems such as high blood pressure, some experts are reluctant to categorize obesity as a disease.

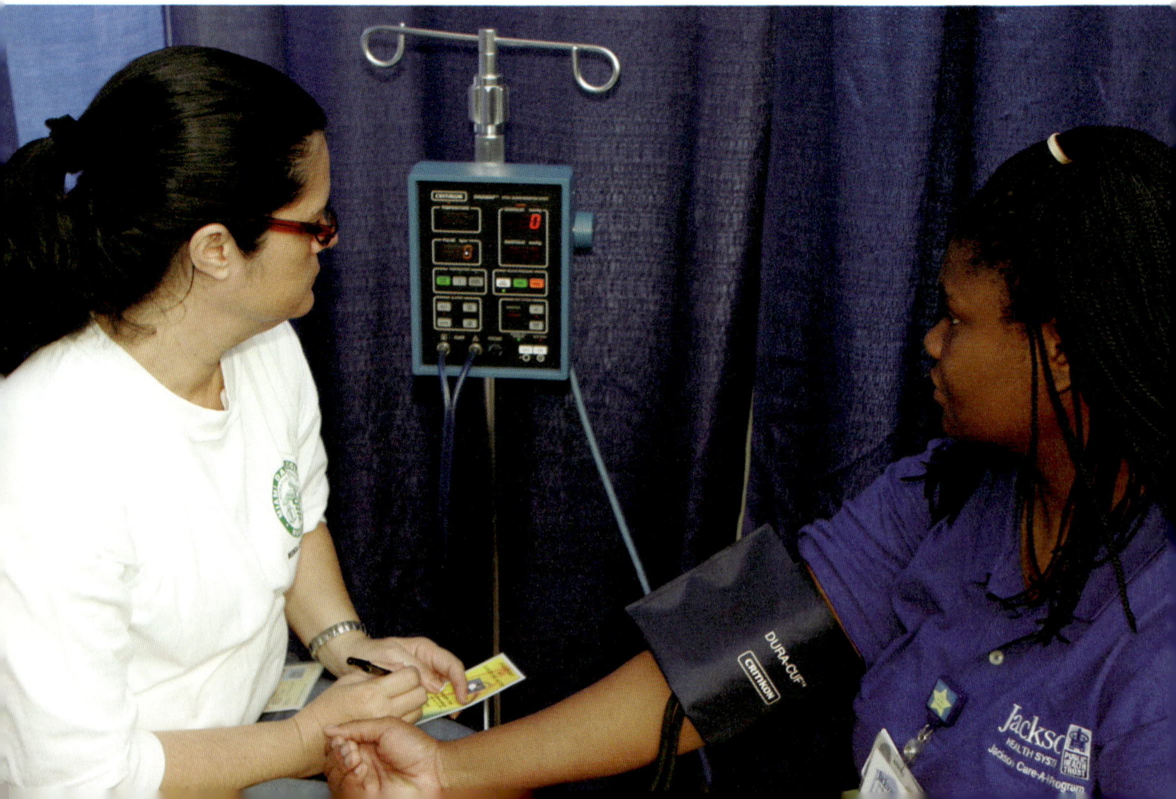

risks such as high blood pressure, hyperinsulinemia, increased cholesterol levels, diabetes, and even certain cancers. However, it is still unclear if obesity is the cause of these risk factors. I believe it is too premature to declare obesity a disease, and that by doing so, it will only make the situation worse.

Why? First, is obesity itself generating the associated health risks? Perhaps obesity is only a marker for poor health but is not the direct cause. Research has not been able to definitively conclude obesity to be the causal factor of its associated negative health outcomes. Research has shown that diet and activity levels, contributors to obesity, are also related to cardiovascular disease, cancer, and strokes despite body weight. In addition, there is strong evidence that overweight, but active individuals, are at a lower risk for cardiovascular disease than thinner counterparts that are not active. In a series of landmark studies at the Cooper Institute, renowned epidemiologist Steven Blair found that the best predictor of mortality was cardiovascular fitness independent of body weight, Body Mass Index (BMI), or % body fat. In other words, an obese person by BMI or % body fat standards that has good cardiovascular fitness is at a significantly reduced risk of all causes of mortality compared to a normal weighted individual that has low cardiovascular fitness. In other words, you can be overweight, or even obese, as long as you have good cardiovascular fitness. It seems that being overweight or obese becomes less of a factor when activity and diet are controlled for, something that most obesity researchers have not considered. More research must be done in order to distinguish the contribution of each before we can clearly say that obesity itself is the culprit.

FAST FACT

According to *The Harvard Medical School Family Health Guide*, about 300 million people are obese worldwide.

Promoting Unhealthy Strategies

By declaring obesity a disease many unhealthy strategies for weight loss (stomach stapling, liposuction, diet pills, body wraps, herbal remedies, etc.) for weight loss might become warranted. Doctors could justifiably use these treatments and feel confident that they are improving the client's health simply by decreasing his or her weight. Pharmaceutical companies would be able to market their quick fix pills and quacks could promote radical diets that promote fast weight loss. It must be emphasized that the effect of these treatments would only be temporary since they don't address long term-behavior change such as lifetime physical activity and improved dietary habits. In addition, even if weight loss is achieved and maintained there is no guarantee that it will be accompanied with health benefits.

Finally, calling obesity a disease will likely promote our nation's preoccupation with weight loss. This would take away from focusing more on the processes of healthy living and would undermine the entire purpose of health promotion. The newly warranted unhealthy weight loss practices would ultimately decrease the public's overall health and would actually drive health care costs up. We must focus not on the product (weight) but on the process (healthy behaviors).

Some worry that calling obesity a disease will make people think there is nothing they can do about their weight and they will reduce their interest in exercising.

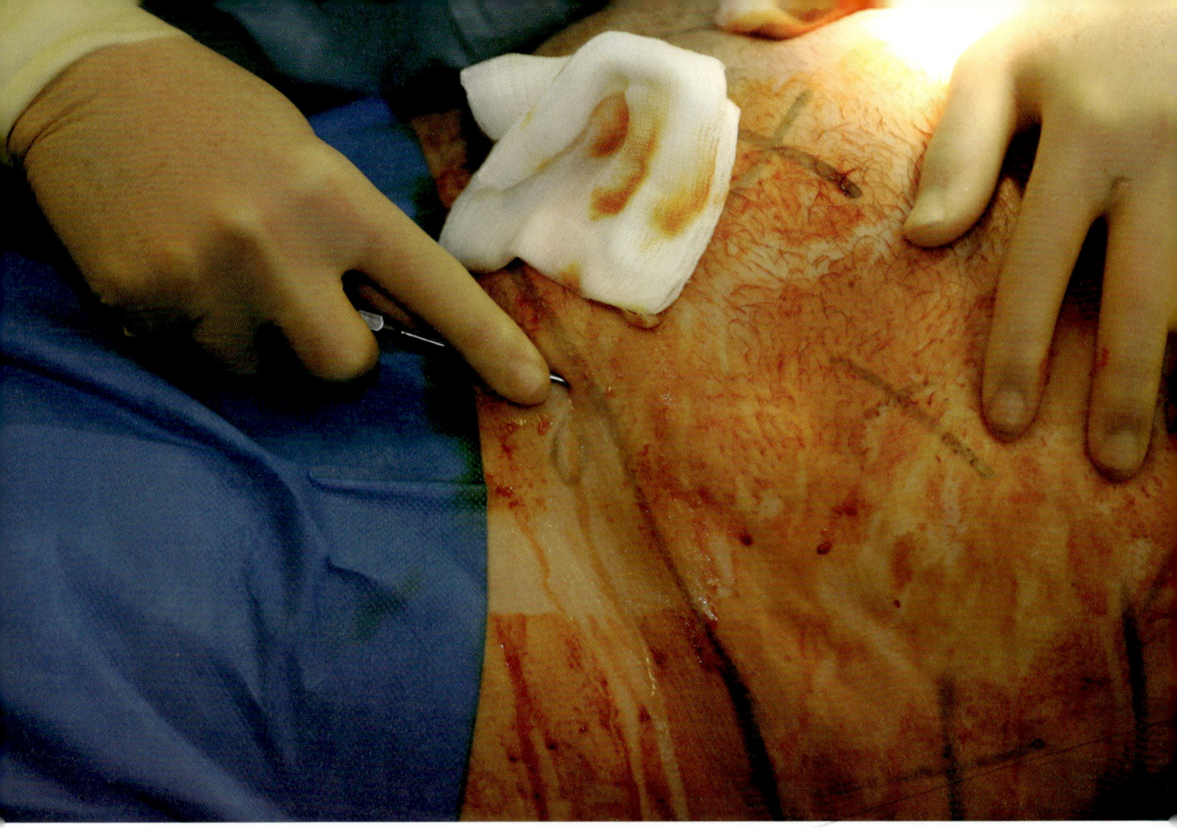

An obese man undergoes liposuction surgery. If obesity were declared a disease, the number of risky weight-loss procedures such as liposuction would likely increase.

We shouldn't be waging a war against obesity but rather a war against inactivity and poor lifestyle choices. Perhaps it would be better to declare inactivity a disease. Maybe this would finally divert attention away from the bathroom scale and help us to start focusing more of our efforts on increasing activity and fitness levels.

EVALUATING THE AUTHOR'S ARGUMENTS:

The author of this viewpoint, Stephen D. Ball, is a nutritionist. The author of the previous viewpoint, Steven Findlay, is an analyst who makes recommendations about what the government should do about health issues. Does knowing the background of these two authors influence the way you interpret their arguments? Explain your reasoning.

Chapter 2

What Are the Causes of Obesity?

An obese man barbeques hot dogs. Debate rages over whether people make themselves obese or junk food and the purveyors of fast foods are the cause of obesity.

Viewpoint 1

Fast Food Makes People Obese

Arne Astrup

"People who often consume fast foods are at high risk of weight gain over time."

The following viewpoint is from the British medical journal the *Lancet*. The author, Arne Astrup, presents the results of a study that concluded that eating fast food is strongly associated with weight gain and changes in how the body processes sugar. Astrup also notes that fast-food serving sizes are much larger than decades ago, and he argues that people eat more because they are served more. He contends that fast-food restaurants should reduce their portion sizes and serve healthier choices.

Arne Astrup is a Danish nutritionist at the Centre for Advanced Food Studies in Copenhagen.

AS YOU READ, CONSIDER THE FOLLOWING QUESTIONS:

1. According to the US CARDIA study cited in the viewpoint, how much weight did individuals who ate at fast-food restaurants more than twice a week gain over individuals who ate at fast-food restaurants less than once a week?
2. According to the viewpoint, what types of habits do individuals who eat frequently at fast-food restaurants tend to have?

Arne Astrup, "Super-Sized and Diabetic by Frequent Fast-Food Consumption?" *The Lancet*, vol. 365, January 1, 2005, pp 4-5. Reproduced with permission from Elsevier.

3. How many times larger are fast-food restaurant portion sizes today than those served fifty years ago, as reported by the author?

Amid the dispute over the realism of the documentary film *Super Size Me*, in which the character, Mr Spurluck, ate McDonald's food three times a day for 30 days and gained 11 kg [24.3 lbs] the report by Mark Pereira and colleagues in [the January 1, 2005,] *Lancet*, adds some scientific evidence to support the film producer's views. The findings from the prospective US CARDIA population study show that frequent fast-food consumption is associated with weight gain and risk of insulin resistance over 15 years.[1] Individuals who ate meals from fast-food restaurants more than twice a week at both baseline and follow-up, gained 4.5 kg [9.9 lbs] more weight and had a 104% greater increase in insulin resistance than individuals who ate less than one meal at a fast-food restaurant each week. The study is the first long-term project to show that people who often consume fast foods are at high risk of weight gain over time, and increase their risk of developing type 2 diabetes.

FAST FACT

Food-industry research results revealed that the number of fast-food restaurants more than doubled from 1972 to 1995. Today there are about 250,000 fast-food restaurants in the United States.

The Link Is Strong

Before the study is embroiled in the dispute between McDonald's and the producer of *Super Size Me*, it is important to note some of its limitations. In the context of a longitudinal observational study, the population size of only 3031 individuals results in modest group sizes for analyses for consistency across sex and ethnic groups. Moreover, the

1. Insulin resistance is a condition in which the body does not respond properly to insulin, a hormone that controls the amount of sugar in the blood.

self-reported information about diet, physical activity, and other lifestyle factors has important inherent errors in measurement, although these errors normally underestimate the strength of the identified associations. . . .

Despite these limitations, most of us would accept that the link between fast foods and weight gain is causal because there are several mechanisms whereby fast foods could produce weight gain. The frequent visitors to fast-food restaurants tended to watch more television, drink more alcohol, consume more fat and energy, drink more soft drinks, and consume less whole-grain products, low-fat milk products, fruit, vegetables, and fibre, which are all habits that will favour a positive energy balance and weight gain. Although the association between fast-food consumption and weight gain was clearly attenuated after adjustments were made for these factors, it still remained significant. So what is it that makes fast food fattening?

The 2004 documentary Super Size Me *investigated the fast food industry's connection to rising rates of obesity in the United States.*

Serving Sizes Have Grown

At least two important features of fast foods were not addressed by the questionnaire in Pereira's study, namely portion sizes and energy density. It is well established that the bigger the portion size provided, the more we consume. And portion sizes of burgers, fried potatoes, pizzas, and soft drinks at fast-food outlets have all increased 2–5 fold over the past 50 years. In addition to large portion sizes, fast food also has high energy density—ie, high kj per 100 g food. [A kilojoule (kj) is a unit of energy. A gram (g) is a unit of mass.] The energy den-

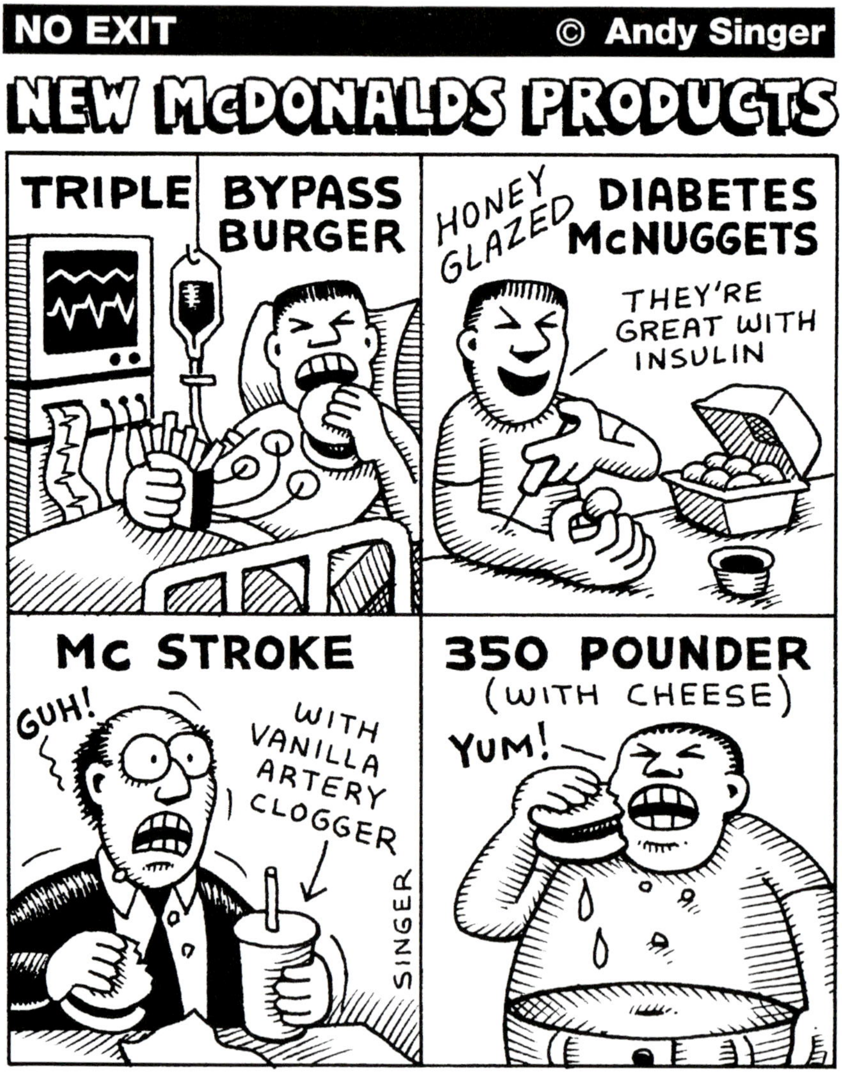

Singer. Reproduced by permission of Cagle Cartoons, Inc.

sity of the entire menu at fast-food outlets is typically about 1100 kj per 100 g. This is 65% higher than the average British diet (about 670 kj per 100 g) and more than twice the energy density of recommended healthy diets (about 525 kj per 100 g). Human beings have only a weak innate ability to recognise foods with high energy density and to down-regulate the bulk eaten to meet energy requirements appropriately.

Make Fast Food Healthier

Fast-food restaurants may argue that the evidence that customers are being super-sized by their meals is too weak. But should customers not be given the benefit of the doubt? Appropriate action would be to reduce portions to normal sizes, and to sell burgers of lean meat, whole-grain bread or buns, fat-reduced mayonnaise, more vegetables, lower-fat fried potatoes, and reduced-sugar soft drinks. Although the price may be increased, at least such changes in fast-food meals can have no adverse health-effects. Recently, some major fast-food companies have taken positive steps by launching new healthier choices, such as porridge for breakfast, and fruit and vegetables for dessert. I hope that this trend continues.

EVALUATING THE AUTHOR'S ARGUMENTS:

The viewpoint you just read states that eating fast food is strongly associated with gaining weight. In the next viewpoint, author Duane D. Freese states that "fast food is not lean and mean . . . it is often packed with calories." With these statements, the authors of each viewpoint appear to agree. Yet they disagree on whether fast-food chains are making people fat. Explain their disagreement.

Viewpoint
2

Fast Food Does Not Make People Obese

Duane D. Freese

"People [want to] blame someone else for their own weight problems."

In the following viewpoint, Duane D. Freese argues that people, not fast-food restaurants, make themselves fat. He discusses a lawsuit in which two teenaged girls sued McDonald's, claiming the chain should be held responsible for their obesity, heart disease, diabetes, high blood pressure, and elevated cholesterol. The girls argued that the fast-food chain failed to obviously display the possible health effects of its food. Freese contends that the lawsuit is nothing more than an attempt to make money off a wealthy business. He admits that much of McDonald's food is calorie laden, but he argues that many other foods are too; McDonald's food is not uniquely dangerous to health. Freese concludes that people are ultimately responsible for their actions, and if they get fat from fast food, it is their own fault.

Duane D. Freese is a writer of news, features, and opinion stories. His work has appeared in the *Saturday Evening Post*, from which this viewpoint was taken.

AS YOU READ, CONSIDER THE FOLLOWING QUESTIONS:

1. According to Freese, what does the lawsuit discussed in this viewpoint require people to believe?
2. According to the author, why would a local candy shop not be sued for making people fat?
3. How much more fat does a Chicken McNugget have than a hamburger, as reported by Freese?

The lawsuit for two obese teenagers against McDonald's—Pelman vs. McDonald's—brings to mind an old Bill Cosby joke.

Nutrition in Chocolate Cake

Cosby is awakened one morning by his tired wife, who tells him to go down and feed the children breakfast. He eventually does, grumpily, and spies a chocolate cake. And his mind goes to the recipe for chocolate cake. There are eggs in chocolate cake. And flour. And milk. There's nutrition in chocolate cake!

So when the kids come down for breakfast, he slices them servings of chocolate cake, and the kids sing in praise of him, until the mother comes down, who has a conniption and sends Cosby back to bed, "where I wanted to be in the first place."

Do we really believe Cosby ever really served the cake, or if he did, he really thought it was nutritious? Of course not. But we suspend our disbelief and go along for the laugh.

Hooked on Burgers or Looking for Money?

The lawsuit against McDonald's requires a similar suspension of disbelief; only, if we go along with it, it threatens to undermine our liberty.

The suit requires us to believe that McDonald's, in essence, hooked the teenagers on their burgers and fries. Obesity is a real health problem. But this case is about trying to make it a bankable one for lawyers.

To do that, they hope people will blame someone else for their own weight problems—in particular, deep-pocket defendants, fast-food chain restaurants such as McDonald's. (You won't see a suit against the local Sweet Shoppe. No money there.)

CLEARLY MY CLIENT WOULD BE SLIM, HEALTHY AND ATTRACTIVE IF MACBURGER HAD ADEQUATELY WARNED HIM OF THE DANGERS OF EATING EVERY SCRAP OF FOOD IN THEIR RESTAURANT.

Haley. www.cartoonstock.com. Reproduced by permission.

"Truths" About Food and Weight We All Know

In the case of fast food, the lawyers have to get around a few facts. One, food in moderation is nutritious and vital. Two, people know when they are gaining weight, and they know that exercise and limiting their calorie intake are the only ways to lose it. Three, they know that fast food is not lean and mean: while it is nutritious, it is often packed with calories. Five, there are numerous alternatives, including eating at home and making your own food.

Accusing "McFrankenstein"

Lawyers in the initial *Pelman* complaint failed to overcome these obstacles to get the federal judge in the case—Robert W. Sweet of the District Court of New York—to suspend his disbelief in their claim.

Unfortunately, though, rather than toss this bad joke of a lawsuit out totally, Sweet gave the lawyers an outline for redrafting it. If McDonald's food could be distinguished from other food as dangerous to health beyond the ken of the reasonable person, well, they might have a case. He even described Chicken McNuggets as a "McFrankenstein creation of various elements not utilized by the home cook," where "it is at least a question of fact as to whether a reasonable consumer would know that a Chicken McNugget provided twice the fat of a hamburger."

Fast Fact

Lunch is the most frequent meal eaten at fast-food restaurants.

And the new complaint follows Sweet's line, right down to attacking Chicken McNuggets.

McDonald's Food No Worse than Many Other Foods

To which, McDonald's should respond with two words: "orange chicken." Or three: "General Tso's chicken." Or two more: "buffalo wings."

The fact is that chicken, in a variety of its appellations, is far more caloric than many of its beefy counterparts.

U.S. Olympic speed-skating medalist Chad Hedrick feasts with friends on Chicken McNuggets. Though McNuggets may be high in calories, it is argued that people have the right to eat whatever food they like.

People choose to dine in fast food restaurants knowing that fast food is not the most nutritious. In doing so, they take responsibility for their food choices.

A cup of orange chicken, according to the *Weight-Watcher's Complete Food Companion*, counts for 13 points on its nutrition scale, versus 11 for a cup of orange ginger beef. General Tso's chicken weighs in at 15 points. And buffalo wings? Just three—and who eats just three?—come in at 9 points. Six Chicken McNuggets count 7. And even within the chicken nugget-strip category, they are less frightening than many other concoctions.

It requires a suspension of disbelief—and total culinary ignorance—to argue that McDonald's has done anything truly strange. And if the lawyers really think they have a better restaurant idea, finance it!

People Are Responsible for What They Eat, Not Restaurants

Instead, the lawyers seek people to suspend their personal responsibility. That's dangerous, for personal responsibility is the foundation upon which all liberty is built.

The punch line to Bill Cosby's joke is that fathers may act dumb, but not be so dumb after all. Cosby got what he wanted: a trip back to bed.

The punch line in the McDonald's lawsuit will be if sly attorneys for the plaintiffs can get a judge and Americans in general to give up another bite of liberty to feed the lawyers' purses. Fortunately, the judge threw out the refiled motion in September [2003], ruling that the plaintiffs could not refile.

The hope here is that people are not so dumb after all, and these cases are sent a permanent rest, where they belong.

EVALUATING THE AUTHOR'S ARGUMENTS:

The author began his essay by telling a joke about Bill Cosby and chocolate cake. Why do you think Freese chose to preface his argument about fast food with this anecdote? Do you think this tactic was effective? Explain.

Viewpoint 3

Junk Food Advertising Promotes Childhood Obesity

"Food and beverage marketing to children in America represents . . . a direct threat to the health of the next generation."

Institute of Medicine

The Institute of Medicine (IOM) advises America on health matters. In December 2005 the IOM reported on the scientific evidence regarding the influence of advertising on the dietary habits of children and teens. It found that the food and beverage industries target children in their advertising, primarily via television. This advertising affects children's food choices, diets, and health, and it is associated with body fat in kids, according to the IOM. The report suggests that the food, beverage, and fast-food restaurant industries should help reduce obesity in children by promoting nutritious foods and beverages.

AS YOU READ, CONSIDER THE FOLLOWING QUESTIONS:

1. How much money is spent per year on advertising food and beverages to children, according to the IOM?

2. During what age range do people develop consumer preferences, as reported by the author?
3. State two of the five conclusions of the IOM report in your own words.

Creating an environment in which children and youth can grow up healthy should be a very high priority for the nation. Yet the prevailing pattern of food and beverage marketing to children in America represents at best, a missed opportunity, and, at worst, a direct threat to the health of the next generation. . . .

Food Advertising Influences Kids

The commercial advertising and marketing of foods and beverages influences the diets and health of children and youth. With annual sales now approaching $900 billion, the food, beverage, and restaurant industries take a central place in the American marketplace. Total marketing investments by these industries have not been clearly identified, although advertising alone accounted for more than $11 billion in industry expenditures in 2004, including $5 billion for television advertising. Television remains the primary promotional vehicle for measured media marketing, but a shift is occurring toward unmeasured sales promotion, such as marketing through product placement [paying a movie or TV show to display a brand-name product], character licensing [using a character such as Scooby Doo to sell a product], special events, in-school activities, and advergames [using video games to promote products]. In fact, only approximately 20 percent of all food and beverage marketing in 2004 was devoted to advertising on television, radio, print, billboards, or the Internet.

Fast Fact

Results of a 2005 study at the University of Illinois at Urbana-Champaign revealed that about 44 percent of television ads aimed at six- to eleven-year-olds are for foods with high sugar content, like soda and candy. Another 34 percent are for snacks and fast-food products.

Children and youth represent a primary focus of food and beverage marketing initiatives. Between 1994 and 2004, the rate of increases in the introduction of new food and beverage products targeted to children and youth substantially outpaced the rate for those targeting the total market. An estimated more than $10 billion per year is spent for all types of food and beverage marketing to children and youth in America. Moreover, although some very recent public announcements by some in the industry suggest an interest in change, the preponderance of the products introduced and marketed for children and youth have been high in total calories, sugars, salt, fat, and low in nutrients.

Advertising Affects Kids Early in Life

How this marketing affects children and youth is the focus of this report. The process begins early in life. Children develop consumer socialization skills as they physically and cognitively mature. Over the

SpongeBob Square Pants is used to help sell Burger King products. Critics complain that pairing cartoons with junk food underhandedly targets young consumers.

span of ages 2–11 years, they develop consumption motives and values as they are exposed to commercial activities; they develop knowledge about advertising, products, brands, pricing and shopping; and they begin to develop strategies for purchase requests and negotiation. The family is the first socializing agent, as parents and older siblings act as sources of information and provide social support and pressure that affect children's behaviors.

Media now have more central roles in socializing today's children and youth than ever before. Advertising and marketing messages reach young consumers through a variety of vehicles—broadcast and cable television, radio, magazines, computers through the Internet, music, cell phones—and in many different venues—homes, schools, child-care settings, grocery stores, shopping malls, theaters, sporting events, and even airports. Virtually all children ages 2–18 years now live in households with a television, and more than half of today's children and youth report that their families have no rules for television viewing. Children and youth under the age of 18 comprise 20 percent of those using the Internet. Myriad marketing approaches are now available, and targeted and integrated marketing has become more prevalent.

Kids Influence Food Purchases

With new outlets, attractions, and tools, children and youth represent a powerful demographic force. Collectively, children and youth spend more than $200 billion annually, and they influence many food and beverage purchases beyond those they make directly. Although children's choices are strongly influenced by their parents and siblings, they are increasingly making decisions at younger ages in the marketplace, either in ways that are independent of parental guidance, or as agents influencing the choices and purchasing decisions of their parents and caregivers. Of the various items that children and youth purchase and influence, food and beverages—particularly candy, carbonated soft drinks, and salty snacks—consistently represent the leading categories.

Young Kids Cannot Tell Ads from Programs

An important issue in discussions about the influence of food and beverage advertising and marketing reaching children and youth relates to the stages of discernment. Before a certain age, children lack the defenses, or skills, to discriminate commercial from noncommercial content, or to attribute persuasive intent to advertising. Children generally develop these skills at about age 8 years, but children as old as 11 years may not activate their defenses unless explicitly cued to do so. Concern about young children's limited ability to comprehend the nature and purpose of advertising, and about the appropriateness or impact of food marketing to which younger children might be exposed, led to a Federal Trade Commission (FTC) rulemaking process in the late 1970s on the question of whether advertising to young children should be restricted or banned as a protective measure. . . .

The question persists, however, about the effects of advertising exposure on children, and . . . to the rapid growth of childhood obesity in the United States.

Worldwide Concern: Kids Vulnerable to Food Advertising

The Committee on Food Marketing and the Diets of Children and Youth was established in 2004. Its charge was to explore what is

Collectively, young people spend more than $200 billion annually, much of it on fast food and beverage purchases.

A Ronald McDonald balloon floats above a busy parade. Children may not recognize this as an advertisement for McDonald's.

known about current food and beverage marketing practices, the influence of these practices on the diets and health of U.S. children and youth, and public and private strategies that have been used or could be used to promote healthful food and beverages choices among children and youth. . . .

The Connection Between Marketing and Body Fatness

The committee's review indicates that, among many factors, food and beverage marketing influences the preferences and purchase requests of children, influences consumption at least in the short term, is a likely contributor to less healthful diets, and may contribute to negative diet-related health outcomes and risks among children and youth. The literature indicates relationships among marketing, dietary precursors, diets, diet-related health, and, in particular, adiposity. . . .

Based on these findings, the committee has identified five broad conclusions. . . .

- Along with many other intersecting factors, food and beverage marketing influences the diets and health prospects of children and youth.
- Food and beverage marketing practices geared to children and youth are out of balance with healthful diets and contribute to an environment that puts their health at risk.
- Food and beverage companies, restaurants, and marketers have underutilized potential to devote creativity and resources to develop and promote food, beverages, and meals that support healthful diets for children and youth.
- Achieving healthful diets for children and youth will require sustained, multisectoral, and integrated efforts that include industry leadership and initiative.
- Public policy programs and incentives do not currently have the support or authority to address many of the current and emerging marketing practices that influence the diets of children and youth. . . .

Healthy Food Should Be Promoted over Unhealthy Food

Central to making progress toward more healthful diets for children and youth will be carefully designed and sustained commitments by the food, beverage, and quick serve restaurant industries to promote the availability, accessibility, affordability, and appeal of nutritious foods and beverages.

EVALUATING THE AUTHOR'S ARGUMENTS:

Think about the food and beverage advertising you see on television. List as many advertisements as you can remember. Do you eat these foods? Do you think the ads influence your choices? Explain your answer.

Viewpoint 4

Junk Food Advertising Does Not Cause Childhood Obesity

"We must resist the urge to look for just one solution for obesity and consider the very urgent need to provide our children with healthy activities."

Carol Glazer

Carol Glazer is the director of the After School Project of the Robert Wood Johnson Foundation (RWJF). The RWJF provides grants to improve health and health care. In the following viewpoint, Glazer argues that although junk food is often blamed for causing obesity in children and teens, the real culprit is a lack of activity among youth. She suggests that after-school programs be pursued to get them off the couch and away from the television. The author concludes that encouraging physical activity and teaching healthy habits can help reduce obesity and provide other long-term positive effects.

AS YOU READ, CONSIDER THE FOLLOWING QUESTIONS:

1. According to the author, how many African American and Latino children are obese?

Carol Glazer, "Obesity Is Not Just About Food," *The Boston Globe*, December 5, 2005, p. A15. Reproduced by permission of the author.

2. What is the After School Matters program in Chicago?
3. What is Capoeira, as described by the author?

Pundits and politicians have homed in on one culprit in the childhood obesity epidemic: fattening food. Despite its obvious sizzle, scapegoating junk food isn't the answer; better school nutrition and less fast food is not the panacea for this public health crisis. A big part of the problem is that many children have very few options after school to do anything other than sit in front of television or computer screens or hang out on their neighborhood streets.

Teens hang out after school, watching TV and drinking sodas. Critics suggest that childhood obesity could be reduced if youth were given more afterschool activity options.

Former president Bill Clinton addresses a gymnasium full of high school students on the importance of eating healthy foods and exercising.

Home Alone and Sedentary

Approximately 5 million children under the age of 12, most of them African-American or Latino, living in poor neighborhoods, spend their time after school home alone. The result is a host of potential problems that compromise their healthy development—social, intellectual, and physical—into adulthood. Among these problems is childhood obesity, which is of epidemic proportions among America's African-American and Latino children, 9 million of whom are now obese.

The effort to ensure that our children live longer and avoid obesity has many voices, including former President Bill Clinton, who recently teamed up with the American Heart Association—and now Nickelodeon—to get the message straight to our youth about the importance of developing healthy eating habits. But if this nation wants to effectively battle the obesity epidemic, we need to look beyond what kids are eating and start considering what happens after the school bell rings. Can we offer them choices that will help them stay safe and physically active, as well as learn social skills and build self-confidence?

Active After School

The very same afterschool programs that provide academic help and cultural enrichment can also counter obesity by encouraging physical activity in a supportive and secure environment. And their impact can be long term: afterschool programs teach young people healthy habits that extend beyond the immediate habits that they will carry with them into the future for a longer, healthier life.

One example of such a program is G-ROW Boston, which provides girls in Boston Public Schools two life-changing opportunities: to learn how to competitively row on the Charles River and apply to

Afterschool activities such as basketball can help counter childhood obesity.

colleges. Launched in 1998, G-ROW aims to diversify the traditionally exclusive sport of rowing and introduce girls to higher education opportunities many never knew were available to them. The staff and coaches build girls' strength and confidence by working with them in the out-of-school hours on the water, in the gym, and in conversations about their future.

> **Fast Fact**
>
> **The American Heart Association recommends that children aged two and older should have at least thirty minutes of moderate-intensity activities every day. They should also have at least thirty minutes of vigorous physical activity at least three to four days each week.**

Get Kids Moving

In Chicago, there is After School Matters, an apprenticeship-based program that offers teens the chance to learn a sport and work within it, such as coaching for soccer and football, swimming well enough to be a lifeguard at the city's public pools in the summer, and other athletic positions. Another program is ABADÁ-Capoeira San Francisco, located in the city's Mission District. The program offers professional instruction of Capoeira, a dynamic Afro-Brazilian art form that combines ritual, self-defense, acrobatics, and music. Using Capoeira as its medium, the program seeks to inspire and empower students, especially youth from disadvantaged backgrounds, to realize their full potential as responsible, confident, productive citizens.

All three programs not only promote health and athleticism but foster healthy relationships between kids and caring adults, helping the kids to gain a sense of belonging and a higher self-esteem.

Creating Solutions to Obesity

Of course, these programs, and others like them, cannot exist without support. Unfortunately, too often a lack of financial, technical, and other support hinders afterschool programs' ability to do more than scratch the surface in the battle against obesity. It is up to leaders and creative thinkers from the realms of education, government, philanthropy, or business to demand or create solutions.

We must resist the urge to look for just one solution for obesity and consider the very urgent need to provide our children with healthy activities that rev up their brains and bodies after the school bell rings. Let's use the opportunities that afterschool programs offer for a brighter, healthier future for all of our kids.

EVALUATING THE AUTHOR'S ARGUMENTS:

The author of this viewpoint argues that when children participate in after-school programs, advertising has little effect on their weight. Think about the after-school programs available at your school. Do any of them help students stay active and healthy? If not, what programs might you recommend to help fellow students lose weight?

Chapter 3

Who Is Responsible for Reducing Obesity?

An obese woman takes a brisk walk for exercise. People question whether the government should promote weight loss—or if people should assume responsibility for their own weight loss.

Viewpoint 1

The Government Should Encourage People to Lose Weight

Penelope Lemov

"States can trace 11 percent of their Medicaid costs to obesity and 5 percent of their overall medical costs to weight problems."

Penelope Lemov writes the health page for *Governing* magazine, whose audience is state and local government officials. In the following viewpoint, Lemov argues that the U.S. government should take a leading role in reducing obesity in America. Obesity is widespread, the health of many is at stake, and state and local governments have seen health care costs increase due to obesity-related illnesses. She concludes that because governments are significantly affected by these problems, they must help tackle them.

AS YOU READ, CONSIDER THE FOLLOWING QUESTIONS:

1. What was the result of the 1978 attempt by the government to ban junk-food advertising?

Penelope Lemov, "The Weight Line," *Governing*, March 2004, p. 49. Reproduced by permission.

2. According to Lemov, what are two reasons why the government should get involved in the American obesity epidemic?
3. What measures has Arkansas taken to reduce obesity, as described by the author?

When the Federal Trade Commission[1] tried to ban the airing of junk-food ads on children's television programs [in 1978] it got its head handed to it. The agency was derided as "the national nanny," and the U.S. Congress threatened to shut it down if it persisted in its anti-advertising campaign.

Americans Are Getting Fatter

That was [about] 25 years and billions of calories ago. But the whole history came back to me recently as states and localities started to weigh in on the latest public health crisis: obesity. It's a problem that's been played up a lot in the press in the past few months and, not surprisingly, a recent poll released by the American Cancer Society and Trust for America's Health [a health advocacy organization] found that Americans now rank obesity as the third-biggest health concern—right after the flu epidemic and cancer.

FAST FACT

According to a 2005 report by Trust for America's Health, Colorado—the leanest U.S. state—pays the least for obesity-related medical costs per person.

Their concerns are warranted. The country as a whole has gotten fatter, with three times the number of obese children as a generation ago. Moreover, more than a quarter of adults are obese, according to a 2002 study by the federal Centers for Disease Control and Prevention [CDC]. In state-by-state rankings, West Virginia and Mississippi residents tip the scale as the heaviest; Colorado's population is the leanest.

1. The Federal Trade Commission (FTC) is an independent agency of the United States government. It reports to Congress. The FTC monitors the buying and selling of goods and services, eliminating unfair or deceptive practices.

A Different Kind of Health Crisis

Crisis though it may be—and certainly, the growing number of overweight schoolchildren is a cause for alarm—obesity is a health problem like few others. There are no vaccinations to give; no tests that can pick up early indicators of the condition. It's not a question of a mosquito-borne virus or contaminated water or unhealthy air—the kinds of things governments can and do take action to control or ameliorate [improve]. For the most part, obesity is dependent on human behavior of a most personal kind: how much and what we eat; how often and how intensely we exercise.

Obesity Is a Growing Problem in the United States

Every state in America has experienced a rise in obesity since 1991.

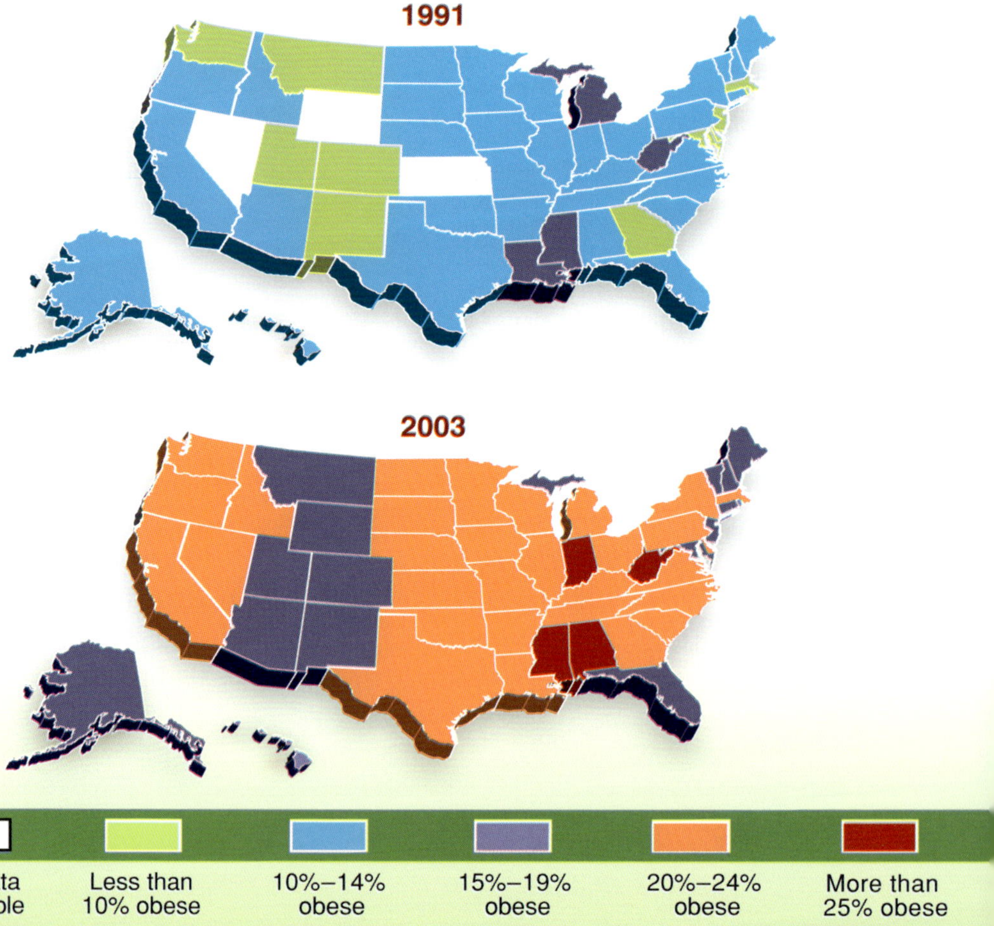

Source: Centers for Disease Control and Prevention.

Darkow. Reproduced by Permission of Cagle Cartoons, Inc.

And that raises the question of whether this is a health problem that calls for governmental action. The line for the FTC's junk-food campaign was tenuous: The agency had children's welfare in mind but, politically, few at that time saw the tie-in as strong enough for the type of intervention the agency advocated.

Governments Pay for Obesity-Related Illness

This time around, though, there is a difference. In addition to their constituents' well-being, states and localities have a fiscal link—an increase in health-care costs since obesity often leads to such chronic illnesses as diabetes, heart disease and several types of cancer. Medicaid and the State Children's Health Insurance Program are directly impacted by that increase in morbidity. A study published recently in *Obesity Research* found that states can trace 11 percent of their Medicaid costs to obesity and 5 percent of their overall medical costs to weight problems. In addition, health insurance premiums—those that governments pay on behalf of their employees and those the private sector offers—also are affected by the increase in disease.

A student selects his lunch from an array of healthy choices. Many schools persist in providing high-calorie, high-fat, and sugar-laden foods in their cafeterias.

Some Governments Are Taking Action

Clearly, states and localities have what lawyers would call "standing" on the issue, and several jurisdictions have begun to experiment with ways to attack the problem. The most obvious is the removal of high-calorie soft drinks and high-fat fast foods from school vending machines and cafeterias. A few school districts around the country have begun taking such measures, and several state legislatures are looking at how to encourage schools to limit vending-machine selections—as well as to increase physical and nutrition education in the schools. Oklahoma's legislature, for instance, will be taking note of a poll taken in December [2003] that showed two-thirds of Oklahomans want soda and candy-carrying vending machines removed and that 84 percent want physical education to be a school requirement.

Arkansas, with 24 percent of its population considered obese—a figure that ranks it as the 6th fattest state in the CDC study—is going further. Governor Mike Huckabee, who lost 75 pounds in the past year, and Fay Boozman, his health director who lost 50 pounds, have put together an initiative to attack the health situation through preventive measures and an insurance plan that would provide incentives for healthy lifestyles. The plan is still in draft form, but among other things, it would offer cash benefits to state employees who lower their blood sugar and cholesterol levels or lose weight.

Denver—capital of a state where only 17 percent of the population is obese—is looking more to exercise than diet. It is engaged in what

Some neighborhoods, such as this one in Stapleton, Colorado, have built exercise paths and nature trails in order to promote healthy, active lifestyles among their residents.

the state's chief medical officer calls "the grand experiment." A new planned community is being developed on the grounds of the old Stapleton airport, an area that sits in the middle of a racially and economically diverse section of the city. The community's design enforces an active lifestyle: lots of parks and trails as well as more reliance on walking to work or taking mass transit. There will also be a flagship health clinic that will emphasize prevention of disease through nutrition counseling and exercise programs.

So far, as governments expand their efforts to reduce obesity, I'm not hearing any mumblings about nannies—national or otherwise.

EVALUATING THE AUTHOR'S ARGUMENTS:

Governments pay health-care costs with money collected from taxpayers. With this in mind, how do you think the government should respond to the obesity crisis? Should it raise taxes to pay for these increased costs? Or should it try to keep costs down and motivate obese persons to lose weight? Explain your answer.

Viewpoint 2

Individuals Are Responsible for Losing Weight

Nick Gillespie

"A skinnier America may well be a healthier America . . . but if it comes into existence through politics rather than individual initiative, choice, and restraint, it will diminish the land of the free."

In the following viewpoint, Nick Gillespie argues that it is not the government's job to make people lose weight. Although the obesity crisis has increased health-care costs, he does not believe this fact gives the government the right to intrude on the personal lifestyles of its citizens. As a solution he suggests that the government reduce the publicly funded elements of health care. Thus, individuals would remain responsible for their weight, their health, and much of the related health-care expenses. He concludes that making the government responsible for peoples' weight loss is inappropriate and un-American.

Nick Gillespie is the editor in chief of *Reason* magazine. *Reason* is a libertarian magazine, meaning that it advocates maximizing individual rights and minimizing the role of government.

AS YOU READ, CONSIDER THE FOLLOWING QUESTIONS:

1. According to Michigan governor Jennifer Granholm, what effect is the obesity crisis having on health-care costs?
2. According to the viewpoint, what percentages of children and adults are overweight in the United States?
3. What is the reasoning behind the author's claim that it is un-American for governments to take action against the obesity epidemic?

When did freedom become just another word for 10 pounds left to lose? "We're just too darn fat, ladies and gentleman, and we're going to do something about it," proclaimed the formerly plus-sized, multiple-chinned Secretary of Health and Human Services Tommy Thompson [in 2004] while announcing a new government ad campaign designed to help citizens shape up. (Thompson has shed an undisclosed number of pounds while on a public diet.)

"We've got so many people who are fat," declared the slender Michigan governor—and former beauty queen—Jennifer Granholm at the

Health and Human Services Secretary Tommy Thompson walks between posters of obese people after announcing a government ad campaign to curb obesity.

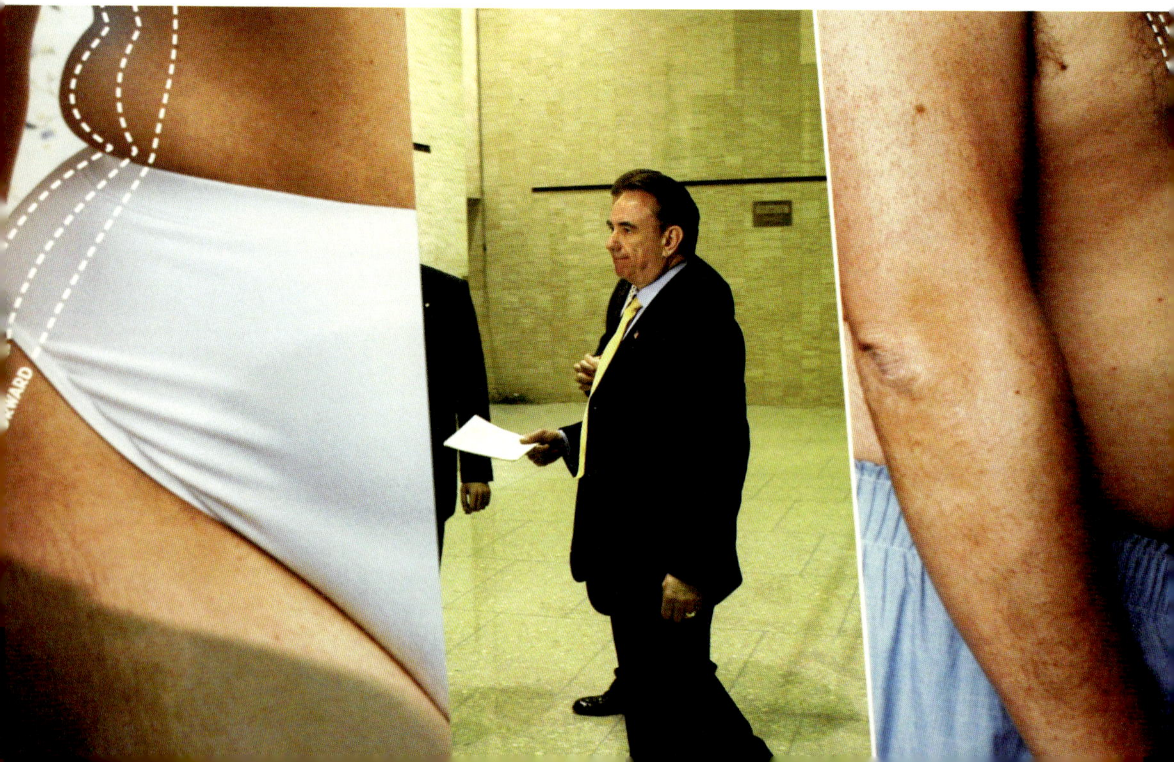

National Governors Association meeting in March [2004]. "And that is really contributing significantly to our health care costs."

Along with more than a dozen of her peers, Granholm strapped on a pedometer to see who walked the farthest during a 16-week period. Other gubernatorial [governor] fat fighters include South Carolina Gov. Mark Sanford (undertaking a 300-mile bike trek), Georgia Gov. Sonny Perdue (publicly forswearing Snickers), and Texas Gov. Rick Perry (sponsoring a 10-kilometer walk/fun run).

FAST FACT

An hour of bicycling, cross-country skiing, swimming, or playing basketball can burn up to 625 calories.

Obesity as a Political Issue?

Thus the United States turns from nation building abroad to nation bodybuilding at home. In a world beset by terrorism, poverty, and malnutrition, who could have imagined that being fat would become the subject not simply of the derision and scorn it has long inspired but a political topic every bit as heartburn-inducing as a Tabasco-flavored Slim Jim?

If history is any guide, it's safe to assume that a hot topic of political discussion will quickly transform into a hot topic of legislation, ranging from Twinkie taxes to mandatory high school exit exams administered by the President's Council on Physical Fitness (which one assumes is now part of the Department of Homeland Security). Can the federal Leave No Chubby Child Behind Act be far away in a country in which 15 percent of kids are officially considered "overweight"? The corresponding figure for adults is about 65 percent, which simply pours more fat on this particular political fire.

Make People Pay for Their Own Health Costs

If being overweight contributes "significantly to our health care costs," the best way to reduce our dangerous dependency on imported stretch fabrics is to make individuals internalize those costs the same way they scarf down the Big Macs and (formerly) supersized fries. That means reducing the publicly funded elements of health care. An added

Michigan governor Jennifer Granholm and other political leaders have made obesity a political issue. Critics argue that it is not the government's job to tell people what to eat or how to exercise.

benefit of that would be to deny politicians—and your taxpaying neighbors—any right to shape your personal lifestyle.

Indeed, there is something creepy and deranged when politicians start calculating versions of a Body Mass Grave Index[1] and flap their gums about the dire need to create a Body Politic by Jake.[2] The current political fixation on fat is as distinctly un-American as Alger Hiss' side job as a Kremlin copyboy.[3] The United States is the most toler-

1. Body Mass Index (BMI) is a value that shows a relationship between weight and height. BMI is used to determine a person's level of body fat and health risk.
2. The author is referring to Body by Jake, a company that produces exercise equipment. Jake gives accompanying fitness advice.
3. Alger Hiss was a United States State Department official who, in 1948, was accused of being a Communist and a spy for the Soviet Union.

ant nation on the planet—as long as you look good in a tight pair of Levi's. So when exactly did freedom become just another word for 10 pounds left to lose?

Let Individuals Choose Fat or Thin

My immigrant grandparents didn't come to this country so that their children, and their children's children, wouldn't have enough to eat. In fact, they left the Old World, with its regular famines and emaciated lower classes, for almost precisely the opposite reason: They dreamed of living in a country where even the masses struggled to squeeze into relaxed fit jeans and size 18 housecoats.

Even as they went to their graves still possessing the lean and hungry peasant bodies they arrived with at Ellis Island, my grandparents must have looked upon the ever larger and fatter bodies of their descendants as the very incarnation of the American Dream.

By injecting politics into diet like so much Bavarian Kreme filling into a Dunkin' Donut, we may well accomplish little more than hardening the arteries of the greatest political experiment of modern times. A skinnier America may well be a healthier America. It will certainly be a more attractive America. But if it comes into existence through politics rather than individual initiative, choice, and restraint, it will diminish the land of the free and the home of the brave in ways that no bathroom scale could ever fully measure.

EVALUATING THE AUTHOR'S ARGUMENTS:

The author of this viewpoint does not believe the government should intervene in the personal issues of its citizens. To what extent do you think that the government should be involved in such issues? Explain your answer and how you would determine where to draw the line at government involvement in citizens' lives.

Viewpoint 3

Gastric Bypass Surgery Helps People Lose Weight

Mitch Stacy

"It's a serious piece of surgery . . . but I felt I had to. I was going to die if I didn't do this."

In the following viewpoint, Mitch Stacy uses research results from a variety of scientific studies to argue that gastric bypass surgery helps people lose weight. Gastric bypass surgery is a procedure in which the stomach is stapled shut so it holds less food. Stacy contends that the procedure can help adults, especially seniors, lose weight and reduce obesity-related health problems such as diabetes and high blood pressure. He argues that the procedure is safe and effective, offering many obese people a new chance at a healthy life.

Mitch Stacy is an Associated Press reporter. The Associated Press is the world's largest and oldest news organization.

AS YOU READ, CONSIDER THE FOLLOWING QUESTIONS:

1. According to the author, how many Americans underwent weight-loss surgery in 2004?
2. How is the word *toboggan* used in the viewpoint?
3. Name three benefits of gastric bypass surgery, as described by Dr. Michal Murr.

Mitch Stacy, "More Obese Seniors Choosing Gastric-Bypass Surgery," Associated Press, September 20, 2005,

With 360 pounds hanging on his 5-foot-7 frame, Robert Stratiff was in sad shape. He had heart problems, poor circulation, wasted knees and sleep apnea that kept him awake most nights. Miserable at age 69, he knew he wasn't long for the world unless he did something drastic. And soon.

So in February 2002, the Colonial Heights, Va., resident had gastric-bypass surgery to lose weight, with Medicare picking up the cost. Because he couldn't eat as much, the weight dropped off faster than he could believe. Exercising got easier.

Now the retired Army colonel who flew helicopters in Vietnam is down to a svelte 170 pounds and swims a mile in the pool four or five times a week to keep fit. He's since had heart bypass surgery and a knee rebuilt. All the other medical problems disappeared with the pounds.

"I knew I was not going to make it if I didn't have that done," Stratiff, now 73, said of the weight-loss surgery. "My health was on a toboggan anyway, and it would have gone down hill quicker. I wouldn't have lived."

Surgeons perform gastric bypass surgery on an obese patient. Such procedures, which reduce stomach size, can help obese people lose drastic amounts of weight.

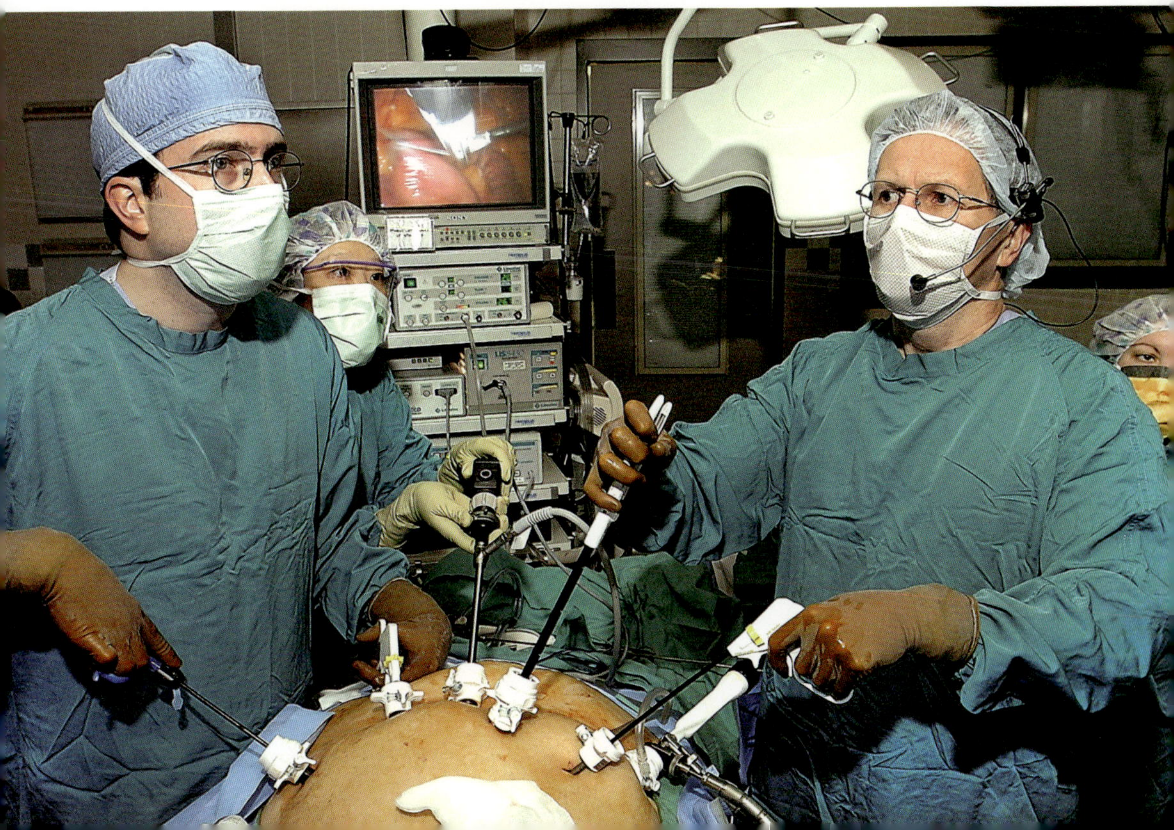

Seniors Benefit from Weight-Loss Surgery

Medical advancements are helping Americans live longer, but a fast-food culture and sedentary lifestyles are making us fatter than ever. People who are morbidly obese—at least 100 pounds overweight—are increasingly opting for some form of gastric-bypass surgery as a last resort.

That includes seniors like Stratiff who are seeking to improve their health and quality of life for the years they have left.

Recent research suggests seniors can benefit from weight-loss surgery as much as younger people and maybe more. One study, from Columbia University's Center for Obesity Surgery in New York, found that patients over 60 got the same benefits from the surgery and had a comparable rate of postoperative complications as younger people.

Risks Low and Benefits High

A soon-to-be published study of 27 gastric-bypass patients 65 and older who had surgery at the University of South Florida and the University of Miami also showed the procedure produced good results

In gastric bypass surgery, the size of the stomach is reduced by stapling off a large section of it. This section becomes unable to hold food. The result makes a person unable to eat as much, and thus lose weight.

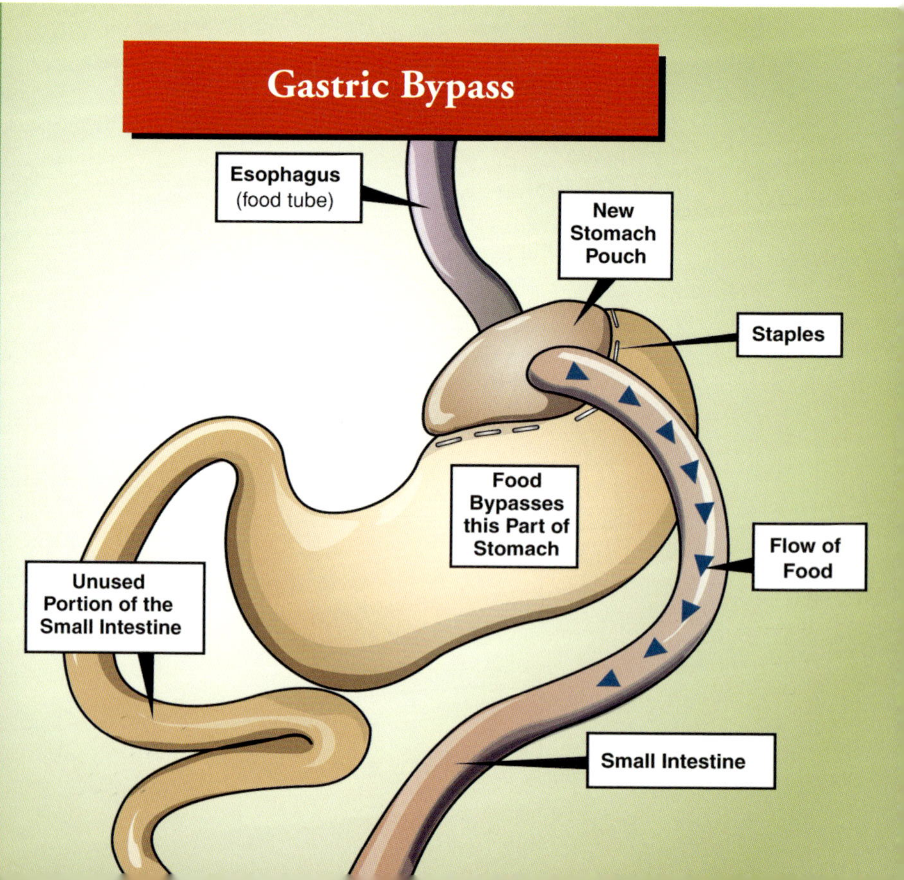

and improved quality of life with about the same rate of mortality and complications as seniors who have heart-bypass and hip replacement surgery. That's a mortality rate of about 2 percent to 4 percent, double the death rate for younger gastric-bypass patients.

"We know it corrects the diabetes, it corrects the hypertension, it takes away the sleep apnea, it fixes the heartburn reflux, it makes their knees and joints last longer," said Dr. Michel Murr, a bariatric [obesity] surgeon at the University of South Florida who has performed nearly 1,000 of the procedures. "All of this is medicine."

FAST FACT

According to the American Obesity Association, morbid obesity affects about 9 million Americans.

"I Was Going to Die if I Didn't Do This"

One of his patients, Sandra Ainbinder of Myakka City near Sarasota, said she weighed a little over 400 pounds when she chose to have the surgery [in 2004] at age 68. She'd lost weight on any number of diets but always gained it back plus more. She was sick, embarrassed and rarely left the house because she could barely walk.

She was rejected by one surgeon because of her age before being accepted by the University of South Florida doctors, with Medicare paying for the surgery.

"It's not a pleasant thing to go through," Ainbinder said. "It's a serious piece of surgery. If there was any other way to do it, I would have done it. But I felt I had to. I was going to die if I didn't do this."

Sixteen months later, Ainbinder is down to 259 and is still losing. Many of her medical conditions either improved or went away. She's got more energy and is looking forward to exercising more after knee-replacement surgery.

"I should be able to join the human race, and I'm looking forward to be being able to walk down the block," she said.

Weight-Loss Surgery Very Popular

The American Society for Bariatric Surgery, based in Gainesville, Fla., said 140,000 people in the United States had some sort of weight-loss

A couple that underwent gastric bypass surgery now fit together inside an old vest that used to fit just one of them.

surgery [in 2004], most of them gastric-bypass—reducing the size of the stomach to limit food intake. The number has grown by about 50 percent a year since 1998.

Doctors estimate that elderly people make up 1 percent to 2 percent of the total, but they expect that percentage to keep growing as Americans live longer and grow larger.

A study [in 2004] in the *Journal of the American Geriatric Society* estimated that obesity in those age 60 and older will increase from 32 percent in 2000 to 37 percent in 2010. Men ages 65 to 74 and women 55 to 64 are the age groups with the highest prevalence of being overweight and obese.

Many private insurance companies cover bariatric surgery, finding it cheaper than long-term treatment of obesity-related health problems, such as diabetes and high blood pressure. Cost of the surgery starts at about $20,000.

Still, the inherent risks in what is indisputably a major operation keep some surgeons from performing the procedure on older people.

Studies Show It Safe and Effective

Armed with the recent studies showing that the surgery is safe and effective for many seniors, the society for bariatric surgery is trying to make it easier for older people to get it. [In 2005], the group petitioned Medicare to develop uniform coverage guidelines and include other types of operations, including less-invasive keyhole surgery that requires only small incisions in the stomach wall.

Medicare coverage of weight-loss surgery currently is decided from region to region. "It's kind of a crap shoot," said Dr. Harvey Sugerman, a past president of the society.

Weight-loss surgery has pitfalls for patients of any age. Recovery can be slow and uncomfortable, and a drastic and permanent change of diet is necessary. Stratiff, for instance, said he hasn't had a French fry since before his operation. He gets sick if he eats anything with too much sugar.

Still, he has no regrets.

"I never look back on the decision and second-guess it," he said. "It was the best thing for me to do. It was the only thing for me to do."

EVALUATING THE AUTHOR'S ARGUMENTS:

The viewpoint you just read argues that gastric bypass surgery helps obese people lose weight. The next viewpoint argues that gastric bypass surgery may not help people lose weight. After reading both viewpoints, what is your opinion of gastric bypass surgery as a weight-loss maneuver?

Viewpoint 4

Gastric Bypass Surgery May Not Help People Lose Weight

"Surgery isn't a quick, easy or even permanent fix."

People

The following viewpoint, taken from *People* magazine, contends that gastric bypass surgery is not a certain solution for weight loss. It uses testimonials—statements from individuals in support of particular facts or claims—to make its case. The viewpoint argues that although some people lose weight immediately after the surgery, they tend to gain it back over time. Because gastric bypass surgery does not fix psychological issues that cause people to gain weight in the first place, the procedure may not be effective in the long run.

AS YOU READ, CONSIDER THE FOLLOWING QUESTIONS:

1. According to the viewpoint, how many Americans have gastric bypass surgery per day?
2. According to Dr. James Ostroff, what percentage of gastric bypass surgery patients regain weight?

"The Pain of Regain After Gastric Surgery," *People*, vol. 16, May 24, 2004, pp. 141–142.

3. How much weight has actress Darlene Cates gained since she had her stomach stapled in 1981?

Gastric surgery—operations that dramatically alter the digestive system, limiting how much food a person can consume or absorb—has become a $3.6 billion industry with an estimated 400 Americans a day going under the knife [in 2004]. For many who struggle with their weight, it seems a miracle cure. But surgery isn't a quick, easy or even permanent fix. "It's a jump start," says Dr. James Ostroff of UC [University of California] San Francisco Medical Center. Patients may lose up to 50 percent of their pre-op weight, but then, estimates Anchorage surgeon John Snyder, about 20 percent will regain a significant amount.

Eating Around the Operation

How? By downing high-calorie liquids like alcohol or milkshakes or snacking continuously. Basically, says Ostroff, "they figure out how to eat around the operation." The one-year mark is a particularly

Five women hug the surgeon who performed their gastric bypass surgery. Though the procedure was effective for them, some bypass patients regain weight.

Englehart. Reproduced by permission of Cagle Cartoons, Inc.

dangerous time. "Hormonal changes following surgery may result in a loss of appetite," says Snyder. "After a dramatic weight loss, the appetite often returns." Above all, surgical procedures do nothing to address patients' emotions, which may compel them to overeat. These women found out that gastric surgery comes with no guarantees.

Stress of Divorce Led to Post-op Weight Gain

Real estate agent Holly Harwig knew she needed help when, meeting with a homeowner in the spring of 1998, she fell right through his wood deck. "I laughed it off," she says. "But inside I was dying." After a workshop with Dr. Daniel Baker, a bariatric [obesity] surgeon in the Minneapolis area, she had bypass surgery and "the weight just fell off," she says. Within 18 months, the 5'1" Harwig, 42, had gone from 285 to 132 lbs. But over the next three years, she added 18 "bounce back" lbs. Then [in 2003], dealing with a difficult divorce, she turned to alcohol and gained 42 more. Although she has now been sober for three months, the weight has stayed put. Harwig, who met third husband Jim, 43, at a bypass-support group in '02, says she's still happier than she was presurgery. "I was a size 28 and now I'm a 16," says the mother of three. "I have to look at that and say, 'Hey, that's really good.' I'm a work in progress."

"I Didn't Know How to Be Thin"

Four months after her surgery in 2000, Beverly Keating no longer recognized herself. "I'd always had a double chin, and it was gone," says Keating, who had lost 108 lbs. from her high of 294. "I could never see my collar bone, and now I could. I could see my cheekbones—I had definition!" Perhaps even better, Keating, 37, no longer suffered from diabetes or asthma. Still, some aspects of the change were difficult. "For someone who's been overweight their entire life, I didn't know how to be thin," recalls Keating, who fluctuated from 250 to 310 even in high school. "Men were taking notice where they didn't before. It was odd and scary." She did what she'd always done when faced with stress: She ate. Her doctor, John Snyder, whose practice is near Keating's home in Anchorage, recommended a post-surgery diet high in protein, with little sugar or dairy, since they make many patients sick. (The self-policing effect usually wears off after about a year.) But Keating, who is married to Doug, a medical biller, and has a son, Eldon, 11, from a previous marriage, "developed my own diet," she says wryly. "I guess that's where I went wrong." Keating's system reacted badly to meats, so she began to graze on cheese and yogurt, snack on bread at her bakery job and drink soda. Over the next two years she added back 54 lbs. to her 5'3" frame, plateauing . . . at 240, where she remains today. "A realistic goal would be to be under 200," she says. "I would have the surgery again if I had to." Still, she knows now that surgery is no cure-all. "To anyone contemplating it, I'd make sure they're prepared for that day when they look in the mirror," she says. "A lot of obese people use fat as a security blanket, and they should make sure they're ready to give it up.". . .

Surgery Cannot Make Old Habits Die

At 512 lbs., Darlene Cates seemed like an ideal candidate for gastric bypass surgery when she appeared as the mother of Johnny Depp and Leonardo DiCaprio in 1993's *What's Eating Gilbert Grape.* In fact Cates, who has since appeared on shows like *Touched by an Angel,* had already undergone another version of the procedure, called stomach stapling, back in 1981. "I thought maybe this was the magic bullet," she says. For a while, it was. She quickly dropped from 412 to 310 lbs. and felt "on air," she says. But her weight loss stalled after a year, and she began putting on pounds. "One day it dawned on me, Wait, I should have been able to eat just a fourth of this burger; how was I able to eat half?" she says. By the mid '80s she was back to her former habits as well as her former weight. "That thing that made you fat in the first place? They don't cut that out during surgery," she says. "The pressures that caused you to seek solace in food are still there when you come home from the hospital." Cates, 56, who lives in Forney, Texas, with husband Bob, a former Marine, now weighs 542 lbs. and relies on a motorized wheelchair to get around. Her daughter Sheri, 38, has been urging her to get a gastric bypass, but Cates worries that she would die on the operating table. "I'm afraid this has become a panacea for everything," says Cates. "'If you're fat, have a gastric bypass.' They don't help people think about the consequences down the road."

EVALUATING THE AUTHOR'S ARGUMENTS:

The viewpoint you just read uses the stories of real people to argue its point. How do these stories affect your opinion of gastric bypass surgery? Do you find them to be good pieces of evidence? Explain your answer thoroughly.

Viewpoint 5

Schools Should Be Responsible for Reducing Childhood Obesity

"School may be the only place where a child tastes healthier choices and learns that intake of some foods ought to be limited."

Howard L. Taras

The following viewpoint contends that schools have a responsibility to combat the obesity epidemic among America's children. Pediatrician Howard L. Taras argues that schools are good places to teach kids about healthy eating habits, but many campuses have become populated by junk food vendors. He suggests that schools implement strategies to combat child obesity, including having better physical education classes, safe bicycle and walking paths, after-school programs that promote physical activity, and improved school nutrition programs.

Howard L. Taras is a member of the American Academy of Pediatrics' Task Force on Obesity.

AS YOU READ, CONSIDER THE FOLLOWING QUESTIONS:

1. According to Taras, what societal changes have occurred in the past few decades that promote obesity?

Howard L. Taras, "A Pediatrician's Prescription to Stem Childhood Obesity," *School Administrator*, vol. 62, October 1, 2005.

2. What percentage of school districts had a contract with a soft drink vendor in 2000, as reported by Taras?
3. What effect does the author say physical activity has on academic performance?

Should school administrators, consumed by woefully underfunded mandates to leave no children behind, be asked to shoulder responsibility for the latest health epidemic in America—childhood obesity?

Obesity Is a Problem for America's Students

Societal changes undoubtedly have contributed to the rise in obesity. High numbers of working parents have little time to cook. Fast-food outlets are ubiquitous. Safety-conscious parents worry about children's unsupervised outdoor play. Cyberspace, virtual reality and thumb games make recreation something done in a seated position. These are only some of the countless potential targets for reversing obesity-causing trends outside of school. So can't we let schools off the hook for this health problem?

School Changes Promote Obesity

The truth is schools also have changed dramatically. How many of us in our 40s or 50s remember drinking sodas in a high school class? The proportion of schools providing daily physical education has plummeted. Exposure in school to colorful, backlit advertisements for high-sugar beverages did not exist until recently.

A national survey by the Centers for Disease Control in 2000 found half of all school districts have a contract with a soft drink distributor. Of these, nearly 80 percent receive a specified percentage of the sales receipts. Almost two-thirds are financially rewarded if sales surpass a minimum amount.

Even though U.S. Department of Agriculture guidelines discourage sales of "foods of minimal nutritional value," 70 percent of schools allow students to buy such snacks during lunch.

Schools' contributions to combating the obesity epidemic are no less critical than those of the public health system or the food and beverage industries. It is the cumulative effect of many changes in children's and adults' environments that is necessary to reverse our current deadly course.

Schools Should Promote Health

The first step schools can take is to implement programs shown through research to work or to be promising. For example, staff development, curricular modification and adequate supplies have been shown to optimize the aerobic quality of physical education class.

Will daily, aerobic physical activity increase test scores? Results of controlled experiments to date do not support this. Yet evidence suggests that supplanting academic time with physical education does not hurt academic performance as measured by cognitive and standardized tests. Immediately after engaging in physical exertion, children

Although the USDA discourages the sale of minimally nutritious foods and sugary drinks in cafeterias, schools can often make large profits by selling them.

Trevor. Reproduced by permission of Cagle Cartoons, Inc.

are more attentive. Increased attention to class content likely counterbalances class time lost to physical activity.

Schools have joined with community partners to arrange for safer bicycle and walking routes to and from school and for healthier afterschool programs that promote physical activity. Schools have hosted community gardens and opened playgrounds on weekends. They have hosted media events to advertise their healthy programs.

We know what it takes to improve the school nutrition program. Food services must be coordinated with students' families (to meet cultural food preferences), the district business office and school health educators. This leads to competitive pricing and income as well as availability of healthier food choices in cafeterias, vending machines, school stores, fund-raising events and classroom celebrations.

Schools Should Set a Healthy Example

Is prohibiting or discouraging students from consuming sugary beverages and fried snack foods at school worth the effort when students may simply consume that much more of these unhealthful products at home and elsewhere? Isn't it going a bit too far to mandate serving mangos instead of pizza or ice cream at a rare classroom celebration?

Actually, these are not unreasonable changes. School may be the only place where a child tastes healthier choices and learns that intake of some foods ought to be limited. Lifestyle improvements that arise from setting a healthy example at school may be delayed for years. But given the dire consequences of inaction, this is an effort schools cannot easily justify denying to today's youth.

EVALUATING THE AUTHOR'S ARGUMENTS:

The author of this viewpoint argues that schools should set a healthy example in the food choices they offer students. Think about what foods are available at your school. Are healthy choices available? If so, what are they? If not, what changes might you recommend your school make?

Viewpoint 6

Parents Should Be Responsible for Reducing Childhood Obesity

"Parents, make the healthy choices: turn off the TV and the video games, go outside with your kids, play ball, go for a walk."

Richard H. Carmona

The following viewpoint is a piece of surgeon general Richard H. Carmona's testimony at a March 2004 Senate hearing on childhood obesity. The surgeon general argues that parents must take responsibility for teaching their children about health. He urges parents to be physically active with their children and help them make healthy food choices. Carmona contends that parents must work together with the government and industry to end America's obesity problem.

Richard H. Carmona became the seventeenth surgeon general of the United States on August 5, 2002.

AS YOU READ, CONSIDER THE FOLLOWING QUESTIONS:

1. According to Carmona, how many servings of fruits and vegetables should young people eat each day?
2. What is "health literacy," as defined by the viewpoint?

Richard H. Carmona, "The Growing Epidemic of Childhood Obesity," www.surgeongeneral.gov, March 2, 2004.

3. In what ways does the author say the food industry could help end the obesity problem among America's youth?

I've traveled the nation talking to students as part of my "50 Schools in 50 States" initiative, and I've seen all kinds of kids. Kids of different races and ethnicities, backgrounds and upbringings. But one thing is constant: too many of them are living unhealthy lifestyles. You can tell just by looking at them. I love seeing their bright smiling faces, full of hope and happiness. But what they don't know about excess weight could end up killing them in a few decades.

We at HHS [United States Department of Health and Human Services] are taking aggressive measures to educate Americans about healthy living and provide incentives to encourage healthy choices. . . .

Parents Should Help Kids Make Healthy Choices

In addition to . . . HHS initiatives and activities, it is very important for parents to take responsibility. We must teach our children to enjoy

Margulies. Reproduced by permission of Cagle Cartoons, Inc.

A family enjoys a healthy, home-cooked meal. Some government and school officials believe it is a family's responsibility to make sure children eat healthy.

healthy foods in healthy portions and encourage them to be physically active for at least 60 minutes a day. The average American child spends more than four hours a day looking at some kind of screen. Parents, make the healthy choices: turn off the TV and the video games, go outside with your kids, play ball, go for a walk. Talk with your kids, spend quality time with them, and when you're together as a family, do something active.

Kids don't automatically know how important it is to be physically active for an hour a day. They don't all know that they need five to nine servings of fruits and vegetables a day. That concept is part of what I'm talking about with Americans of all ages: increasing our health literacy.

Health literacy is the ability to access, understand, and use health-related information and services to make appropriate health decisions. We must close the gap between what health professionals know and what parents and children understand about physical activity and healthy eating.

Every morning people wake up and, while they're sitting at the kitchen table, they read the newspaper and the cereal box. Throughout the day they read the nutritional information on their meals and on their snacks. But do they really understand the information they're reading? Can parents explain it to their children, who see tantalizing "kid food" products that they don't know are loaded with sugar and fat?

Food Labeling Can Help Educate

To make healthy choices, parents and children need easy-to-understand information that fits into their busy lifestyles. Many people, even educated Americans, don't know what a calorie is, or how to burn it. It's our job to make that kind of health information meaningful and helpful. For example, Secretary Tommy Thompson [of the HHS] recently announced that food labels will list trans fat content. This will give American families information to make smart choices to lower their intake of these unhealthy fats.

I ask you to work with the President, the Secretary, and me, as well as every mom and dad in America, to promote healthy living, improve health literacy, and encourage healthier lifestyles so that we can end our nation's obesity problem before it has a chance to reach into another generation of Americans. Working together, industry, government, and individuals can achieve these goals.

Fast Fact

According to a 2003 study by the Kaiser Family Foundation, children aged six months to six years spend an average of two hours each day using screen media. These activities provide a low level of physical activity.

The Food Industry Can Help Provide Healthy Choices

Industry can help by providing healthier choices for customers and including better information about its products. Secretary Thompson is working with industry to assure that healthy choices are developed and made available to all Americans.

A mother reads a food can label with her daughter. Teaching children about nutrition while they are young can help them make smart choices about food for the rest of their lives.

Scientific leaders in government and the private sector need to make sure that people have accurate, science-based information about the factors that contribute to overweight and obesity. This testimony has outlined for you HHS' efforts to combat the obesity epidemic.

Most importantly, parents need to be good role models by being physically active and by encouraging their children to exercise and make healthy choices about what they eat and how much they eat.

EVALUATING THE AUTHOR'S ARGUMENTS:

This chapter presented different answers to the question "Who is responsible for reducing obesity?" Based on the information in this chapter, make a list of those responsible for reducing obesity. Put who you think is the most responsible party first and the least responsible last. Explain the rationale for each of your rankings.

Facts About Obesity

Editor's note: These facts can be used in reports or papers to reinforce or add credibility when making important points or claims.

Defining Obesity

- The Centers for Disease Control and Prevention (CDC) defines the terms *obesity* and *overweight* as "ranges of weight that are greater than what is generally considered healthy for a given height."
- For adults, overweight and obesity ranges are defined by the body mass index (BMI). The BMI is calculated using a person's weight and height. An adult with a BMI between 25 and 29.9 is considered overweight. An adult with a BMI of 30 or higher is considered obese, and those with 40 or more are severely obese.

Obesity in America

According to the American Obesity Association:

- Approximately 127 million adults in the United States—about 43 percent of the population—are overweight or obese.
- Of the obese, about 9 million are severely obese.
- The number of overweight and obese adults in all age groups and in both genders has increased since the last decade.
- Among men, those aged sixty-five to seventy-four years have the highest prevalence of being overweight and obese. Among women, those aged fifty-five to sixty-four years have the highest prevalence.
- More men than women are overweight.
- More women than men are obese.
- Obesity is higher among persons with less education and lower among persons with more education.
- Over the past two decades, obesity has increased in all regions of the United States.

- Regionally, the percentage of obese adults is highest in the eastern south-central United States (Alabama, Kentucky, Mississippi, Tennessee) and lowest in New England (Connecticut, Massachusetts, Maine, New Hampshire, Rhode Island, Vermont).
- According to the Organization for Economic Cooperation and Development (OECD), the daily caloric intake of Americans grew nearly 25 percent between 1973 and 1999.
- According to the American Heart Association, each year an estimated three hundred thousand American adults die of causes related to obesity.
- A study published in the *Journal of Human Resources* in 2004 revealed that obese white American women make 9 percent less wages or earnings than do nonobese white American women.

Obesity Around the World

According to the World Health Organization (WHO):

- Obesity is a global epidemic for both children and adults.
- Globally, there are more than 1 billion overweight adults. At least 300 million of these overweight adults are obese.
- Approximately 22 million children under five are estimated to be overweight worldwide.
- Obesity rates have risen threefold or more since 1980 in some areas of North America, the United Kingdom, eastern Europe, the Middle East, the Pacific Islands, Australia, and China.

According to the OECD:

- The worldwide incidence of weight-related problems is the highest ever recorded.
- The United States (65 percent), Mexico (62 percent), and Great Britain (60 percent) are, respectively, the first, second, and third fattest countries.
- Australia and the Slovak Republic are the fourth and fifth fattest nations, each with about 57 percent of their population overweight and obese.
- Countries with more females working outside the home are more likely to have weight-related problems.

Obesity and Children

- According to University of Michigan pediatrician Joyce Lee, obese children have more than twice the chance of having diabetes compared with children of normal weight.
- The National Heart, Lung, and Blood Institute reports that overweight children are more likely to become overweight or obese as adults.

Children who have the following characteristics are at increased risk for obesity:

- lack of regular exercise
- high frequency of watching television and using computers
- overconsumption of high-calorie foods
- nonworking, obese, and overweight parents
- low family incomes

The Obesity Action Coalition reports:

- Among children and teens aged six to nineteen years, 16 percent (more than 9 million) are considered overweight or obese. This number has more than tripled since 1980.
- Children who are considered obese are 70 percent more likely to continue being obese into adulthood.
- Obese children are at greater risk for serious medical issues such as heart disease, high cholesterol, high blood pressure, diabetes, sleep apnea, and cancer.

The 2000–2001 Canadian Community Health Survey data revealed:

- Girls who were former smokers had a higher risk of being obese than those who had never smoked.
- Boys who were physically inactive or just moderately active had a higher risk of being obese than boys who had higher levels of activity.
- Girls who lived with an obese parent were six times more likely to be obese than were girls who did not live with an obese parent.
- Boys who lived with an obese parent were nearly three times more likely to be obese than were boys who did not live with an obese parent.

The Health Effects of Obesity

According to the CDC:

- The risk of diabetes, heart disease, stroke, high blood pressure, and osteoarthritis increases dramatically when one is overweight or obese.
- Obesity is associated with cancers of the esophagus, breasts (in both men and women), large intestine, kidneys, and endometrium (lining of the uterus).

The American Diabetes Association reports:

- Nearly nine out of ten people with newly diagnosed type 2 diabetes are overweight.
- At least one out of every five overweight people has several metabolic problems that together can lead to serious complications such as heart disease.
- In the analyses carried out for the WHO *World Health Report 2002*, approximately 58 percent of diabetes, 21 percent of heart disease, and 8 to 42 percent of certain cancers globally were attributable to individuals being overweight or obese.

Organizations to Contact

American Cancer Society (ACS)

(800) 227-2345
www.cancer.org

The American Cancer Society, with thousands of local offices throughout the United States, is a volunteer health organization whose mission is to eliminate cancer as a major health problem. Obesity is associated with many cancers, such as those of the breasts, esophagus, large intestine, and kidneys. The ACS provides information on obesity and cancer. It offers articles such as "Obesity Linked to All Types of Breast Cancer," "Obesity Linked to Cancer—Other Chronic Disease Risk," and "Studies Help Clarify Link Between Obesity and Prostate Cancer." It also has obesity-related Web pages such as "Take Control of Your Weight."

American Diabetes Association (ADA)

1701 N. Beauregard St.
Alexandria, VA 22311
(800) 342-2383
e-mail: askada@diabetes.org
www.diabetes.org

The American Diabetes Association, a not-for-profit health organization, works to prevent and cure diabetes. The ADA works to educate people about weight-related issues because approximately 90 percent of persons newly diagnosed with type 2 diabetes are overweight or obese. As a part of its program, the ADA provides many tip sheets about obesity on its Web site, including "Losing Weight: What Does It Take?" "Be Active: But How?" and "Food and Portion Size."

American Heart Association (AHA)

7272 Greenville Ave.
Dallas, TX 75231

800) 242-8721
www.americanheart.org

The mission of the American Heart Association is to reduce disability and death from cardiovascular diseases and strokes. This volunteer health organization has published a scientific position paper on obesity since it is a major risk factor for coronary heart disease. In addition, the AHA has related scientific position papers and articles on its Web site, including "Obesity and Cardiovascular Disease," "Overweight in Children and Adolescents," and "Clinical Implications of Obesity with Specific Focus on Cardiovascular Disease."

American Obesity Association
1250 Twenty-fourth St. NW, Suite 300
Washington, DC 20037
202) 776-7711
www.obesity.org

The American Obesity Association was founded to combat obesity and its health effects. It accomplishes this mission by educating the public about obesity and its association with illness and by promoting obesity research. It also helps protect consumers from diet frauds and scams.

American Society of Bariatric Physicians (ASBP)
2821 S. Parker Rd.
Aurora, CO 80014
(303) 770-2526
fax: (303) 779-4834
e-mail: info@asbp.org
www.asbp.org

Bariatrics is the medical treatment of obesity and related conditions. The purpose of the American Society of Bariatric Physicians is to support member physicians who treat overweight and obese patients. The ASBP provides information on recent developments in the field of obesity to its members and supports public policies to prevent obesity. The ASBP also provides information on obesity and weight loss to the public.

Centers for Disease Control and Prevention (CDC)
Division of Nutrition and Physical Activity (DNPA)

4770 Buford Hwy. NE, MS/K-24
Atlanta, GA 30341-3717
(770) 488-5820
e-mail: cdcinfo@cdc.gov
www.cdc.gov/nccdphp/dnpa

The CDC is part of the National Institutes of Health, Department of Health and Human Services. Its Division of Nutrition and Physical Activity has three focus areas: nutrition, physical activity, and overweight and obesity. The DNPA addresses the role of nutrition and physical activity in improving the public's health. DNPA activities include health promotion, research, training, and education. The DNPA maintains an overweight and obesity Web page, on which it provides research-based information for consumers.

Cleveland Clinic Bariatric and Metabolic Institute (BMI)
9500 Euclid Ave.
Cleveland, OH 44195
(800) 223-2273, ext. 52224
e-mail: weight_mgmt_program@ccf.org
http://cms.clevelandclinic.org/bariatricsurgery

The BMI provides weight-loss surgery, nutritional guidance, and support programs for its patients. It is part of the Cleveland Clinic, a not-for-profit multispecialty academic medical center.

International Association for the Study of Obesity (IASO)
231 N. Gower St.
London, UK
NW1 2NR
telephone: +44 20 7691 1900
e-mail: enquiries@iaso.org
www.iaso.org/www.iotf.org

The IASO is a nongovernmental organization with forty-nine member associations representing fifty-three countries. The mission of the IASO is to improve global health by promoting the understanding of obesity and weight-related diseases through scientific research and discussion. The IASO works with the World Health Organization and other global nongovernmental organizations toward this goal.

National Heart, Lung and Blood Institute (NHLBI)

Building 31, Room 5A48, 31 Center Dr. MSC 2486
Bethesda, MD 20892
(301) 592-8573
e-mail: nhlbiinfo@nhlbi.nih.gov
www.nhlbi.nih.gov

The NHLBI is part of the National Institutes of Health. It leads a national program in diseases of the heart, blood vessels, lungs, and blood. The institute plans, conducts, and supports research and education projects. The NHLBI also conducts educational activities for health professionals and for the public. In addition, it provides educational materials on obesity and physical activity, focusing on both children and adults.

North American Association for the Study of Obesity (NAASO)

8630 Fenton St., Suite 918
Silver Spring, MD 20910
(301) 563-6526
www.naaso.org

The NAASO encourages research into the causes and treatment of obesity. This scientific society informs the medical community and the public of advances in these areas. The mission of the NAASO also includes education and advocacy to help improve the lives of those who are obese.

Obesity Action Coalition (OAC)

4511 N. Himes Ave., Suite 250
Tampa, FL 33614
(800) 717-3117
e-mail: info@obesityaction.org
www.obesityaction.org

The Obesity Action Coalition is a not-for-profit organization that educates not only obesity patients but also their family members and the public. It provides links to resources and obesity support groups throughout the United States. The OAC works against the negative stigma of obesity and is an advocate for safe and effective obesity treatment.

The Obesity Awareness and Solutions Trust (TOAST)

The Latton Bush Centre, Southern Way, Harlow
Essex, UK
CM18 7BL
telephone: +44 1279 866010
e-mail: enquiries@toast-uk.org.uk
www.toast-uk.org.uk

TOAST promotes the idea that obesity is a complex problem with no single solution. It asserts that the treatment and prevention of obesity must go beyond the medical model of diet, exercise, and medication.

Overeaters Anonymous (OA)

World Service Office
PO Box 44020
Rio Rancho, NM 87174-4020
(505) 891-2664
e-mail: info@oa.org
www.oa.org

Overeaters Anonymous is an organization open to individuals recovering from compulsive overeating. Individuals share their experiences and support each other to stop eating compulsively. OA provides a twelve-step program, modeled after the twelve-step program of Alcoholics Anonymous, to help members control their food addictions. Members can attend meetings in their own localities and can communicate with members worldwide via the Internet.

Shape Up America!

e-mail: info@shapeup.org
www.shapeup.org

Shape Up America! is a not-for-profit organization founded by former U.S. surgeon general C. Everett Koop. Its mission is to educate the public on how to achieve and maintain a healthy weight. Shape Up America! focuses on behavioral change, encouraging increased physical activity, and healthy eating.

Take Off Pounds Sensibly (TOPS)

e-mail: topsinteractive@tops.org

www.tops.org

TOPS is an international not-for-profit weight-loss support group. There are ten thousand chapters worldwide. The mission of TOPS is to support members' efforts to lose weight. The organization uses experts in the field of medical research, nutrition, fitness, and psychology to support its volunteer chapter leaders.

For Further Reading

Books

Frances M. Berg, *Underage and Overweight: America's Childhood Obesity Crisis; What Every Family Needs to Know*. Long Island City, NY: Hatherleigh, 2005. Written by a childhood obesity expert, this book proposes that children work to maintain their weight as they grow older.

Paul Campos, *The Obesity Myth: Why America's Obsession with Weight Is Hazardous to Your Health*. New York: Gotham, 2004. Argues that America's obesity epidemic is overblown, suggesting that the diet industry perpetuates the myth of an epidemic for its own gain.

Greg Critser, *Fat Land: How Americans Became the Fattest People in the World*. New York: Houghton Miflin, 2003. Chronicles the development of high-fructose corn sweetener and palm oil, which are incorporated into a wide variety of foods. Argues that these products trigger fat storage and have contributed to the obesity epidemic. Discusses how the poor become the fattest, primarily due to a lack of awareness.

Michael Gard and Jan Wright, *The Obesity Epidemic: Science, Morality, and Ideology*. New York: Taylor & Francis, 2005. Discusses the cultural, political, and social issues surrounding obesity.

Institute of Medicine, *Preventing Childhood Obesity: Health in the Balance*. Washington, DC: National Academies Press, 2005. Report from the institute's Committee on Prevention of Obesity in Children and Youth. It examines the nature, extent, and consequences of obesity in American children and adolescents.

———, *The Richard and Hinda Rosenthal Lectures 2004: Perspectives on the Prevention of Childhood Obesity in Children and Youth*. Washington, DC: National Academies Press, 2006. A panel discussion on the institute's report "Preventing Childhood Obesity: Health in the Balance." It provides an overview and framework for preventing childhood obesity, a government perspective, and an industry perspective. It concludes with a discussion of the various perspectives of the problem.

Francine R. Kaufman, *Diabesity: What You Need to Know If Anyone You Care About Suffers from Weight Problems, Pre-Diabetes, or Diabetes.* New York: Bantam, 2006. Written by the past president of the American Diabetes Association, this book discusses the connection between diabetes and obesity.

J. Michael McGinnis et al., eds., *Food Marketing to Children and Youth: Threat or Opportunity?* Washington, DC: National Academies, 2006. Focuses on what impact food and beverage marketing has had on the dietary patterns and health status of American children.

Mary P. McGowan with Jo McGowan Chopra, *Gastric Bypass Surgery.* New York: McGraw Hill, 2004. Discusses the pros and cons of this surgical weight-loss treatment.

Susan Okie, *Fed Up! Winning the War Against Childhood Obesity.* Washington, DC: Joseph Henry, 2005. Contains case studies that chronicle contributing factors to childhood obesity.

J. Eric Oliver, *Fat Politics: The Real Story Behind America's Obesity Epidemic.* New York: Oxford University Press, 2005. Argues that America's obesity epidemic is largely the creation of doctors, politicians, and health officials who have ties to the diet and drug industry.

Sylvia B. Rimm with Eric Rimm, *Rescuing the Emotional Lives of Overweight Children: What Our Kids Go Through—and How We Can Help.* Emmaus, PA: Rodale, 2005. Written by a family psychologist and based on a national survey of middle-school children, personal interviews, case studies, and other international research. Helps readers understand the psychological well-being of overweight children. Provides a six-step plan to help overweight children acquire a healthier lifestyle.

Eric Schlosser, *Fast Food Nation: The Dark Side of the All-American Meal.* New York: Houghton Mifflin, 2001. Sketches the development of the fast-food industry in the United States. Argues that the fast-food industry encourages obesity with high-calorie, high-fat food, especially for young people.

Periodicals and Reports

Gary Andres, "The Waistline Wars," *Washington Times*, April 20, 2005.

Matthew Boyle, "Can You Really Make Fast Food Healthy?" *Fortune*, August 9, 2004.

Kelly D. Brownell, "Fast Food and Obesity in Children," *Pediatrics*, January 2004.

Glenn Cook, "Killing PE Is Killing Our Kids the Slow Way," *American School Board Journal*, October 2005.

Helen Cordes, "Fat Cities: How Modern Life Encourages Obesity and What We Can Do About It," *Sierra*, January/February 2005.

Sarah Ellison and Janet Adamy, "Panel Faults Food Packaging for Kid Obesity," *Wall Street Journal*, December 7, 2005.

Katherine M. Flegal et al., "Excess Deaths Associated with Underweight, Overweight, and Obesity," *Journal of the American Medical Association*, April 20, 2005.

Kevin R. Fontaine et al., "Years of Life Lost Due to Obesity," *Journal of the American Medical Association*, January 8, 2003.

Adrienne Forman, "When Diets Don't Work: Losing Weight with Drugs, Surgery," *Environmental Nutrition*, July 2005.

W. Wayt Gibbs,"Obesity: An Overblown Epidemic?" *Scientific American*, June 2005.

Gina Kolata, "Data on Deaths from Obesity Is Inflated, U.S. Agency Says," *New York Times*, November 24, 2004.

Fred Kuchler, "Taxing Snacks to Reduce Obesity," *Amber Waves*, November 2004.

Alison McCook, "Supersize Controversy," *Current Health*, October 2004.

Marianne McGinnis, "Hold the Sugar," *Prevention*, January 2005.

Jennifer Ordoñez, "Fast-Food Lovers, Unite!" *Newsweek*, May 24, 2004.

S. Jay Olshansky et al., "A Potential Decline in Life Expectancy in the United States in the 21st Century," *New England Journal of Medicine*, March 17, 2005.

Stephen Perrine et al., "How the Low-Carb Craze Is Making Us Fat," *Men's Health*, May 2004.

Gary Ruskin and Juliet Schor, "Junk Food Nation: Who's to Blame for Childhood Obesity?" *Nation*, August 29–September 5, 2005.

Rebecca Skloot, "Flabby Coverage," *Popular Science*, July, 2005.

Amanda Spake, "Learning About Fat," *U.S. News & World Report*, October 11, 2004.

Rob Stein, "Can Being Fit Outweigh Fat? It's Possible to Be Obese and Healthy, Experts Say," *Washington Post*, November 26, 2004.

Jacob Sullum, "The War on Fat," *Reason*, August/September 2004.

U.S. Government Accountability Office, *Childhood Obesity: Most Experts Identified Physical Activity and the Use of Best Practices as Key to Successful Programs*, October 7, 2005.

Kathleen Vail, "Raising the (Salad) Bar on Obesity," *Education Digest*, March 2004.

Jayachandran N. Variyam, "Overweight Children: Is Parental Nutrition Knowledge a Factor?" *Food Review*, May/August 2001.

Monica Hobbs Vinluan, "Reducing Obesity Through Recreation," *Parks & Recreation*, October 2005.

Lisa R. Young and Marion Nestle, "The Contribution of Expanding Portion Sizes to the US Obesity Epidemic," *American Journal of Public Health*, February 2002.

Web Sites

Centers for Disease Control and Prevention: Overweight and Obesity (www.cdc.gov/needphp/dnpa/obesity/). The CDC's Web site on overweight and obesity provides selected resources, such as information on how to achieve and maintain a healthy weight, and dietary guidelines for Americans.

Medline Plus: Obesity (www.nlm.nih.gov/medlineplus/obesity.html). The U.S. National Library of Medicine and the National Institutes of Health provide Medline Plus, an information Web site on health topics. The obesity Web page provides links to obesity-related news reports and information from the National Institutes of Health and other national and prestigious health-related institutions and organizations. It also provides links to information on treatment, prevention, screening, financial issues, clinical trials, research, organizations, and more.

The Surgeon General's Call to Action to Prevent and Decrease Overweight and Obesity (www.surgeongeneral.gov/topics/obesity). This Web site provides the surgeon general's full report and fact sheets. The Web site also includes links to the report "Healthy People 2010: Leading Health Indicators" and overweight and obesity information related to that report.

Weight-Control Information Network (http://win.niddk.nih.gov). This Web site is an information service of the National Institute of Diabetes and Digestive and Kidney Diseases. It provides science-based and up-to-date information on weight control, obesity, physical activity, and related nutritional issues.

World Health Organization: Obesity (www.who.int/topics/obesity/en). The World Health Organization is the health agency of the United Nations. Its Web site on obesity has links to news, reports, activities, and events on this topic.

Index

Picture Credits

Cover: © Dennis MacDonald/Alamy
© Alex Segre/Alamy, 14
Alex Wong/Getty Images News/Getty Images, 23, 74, 76
© Andrew Holbrooke/CORBIS, 34
Associated Press, 33, 43, 50, 57, 70, 71, 79, 82, 85
© Brigitte Sporrer/zefa/CORBIS, 11
© C. Devan/zefa/CORBIS, 60
© Cathrine Wessel/CORBIS, 62
© Don Mason/CORBIS, 98
Getty Images Publicity/Getty Images, 49
© Jeff Greenberg/Alamy, 36
© Karen Kasmauski/CORBIS, 17
© Kelly-Mooney Photography/CORBIS, 10
Larry W. Smith/Getty Images News/Getty Images, 54
© Matthew Totton/Alamy, 39
Maury Aaseng, 18, 26, 68, 80
© Max Morse/Reuters/CORBIS, 27
© Michael A. Keller/zefa/CORBIS, 20
© Najlah Feanny/CORBIS, 30
Photos.com, 56
© PhotoStockFile/Alamy, 38
© PNC/zefa/CORBIS 16, 40
© Robin Nelson/Alamy, 65
© Ronnie Kaufman/CORBIS, 96
Spencer Platt/Getty Images News/Getty Images, 61
Tim Boyle/Getty Images News/Getty Images, 91

About the Editor

Sandra Alters holds a Ph.D. degree in science education and a Master's degree in biology. Formerly of the University of Missouri-St. Louis and Salem State College (Massachusetts), Dr. Alters has authored many articles in professional literature, over sixty chapters and features in books, a laboratory manual, a children's science book, and several textbooks. Her textbooks include *Essential Concepts for Healthy Living* (with Wendy Schiff, Jones and Bartlett Publishers, © 2006) and *Biology: Understanding Life* (with Brian Alters, John Wiley & Sons, © 2006). She and her husband Brian live in Montreal, Quebec.